STRIKE & SCORE
RED CARD ROMANCE

MADI DANIELLE

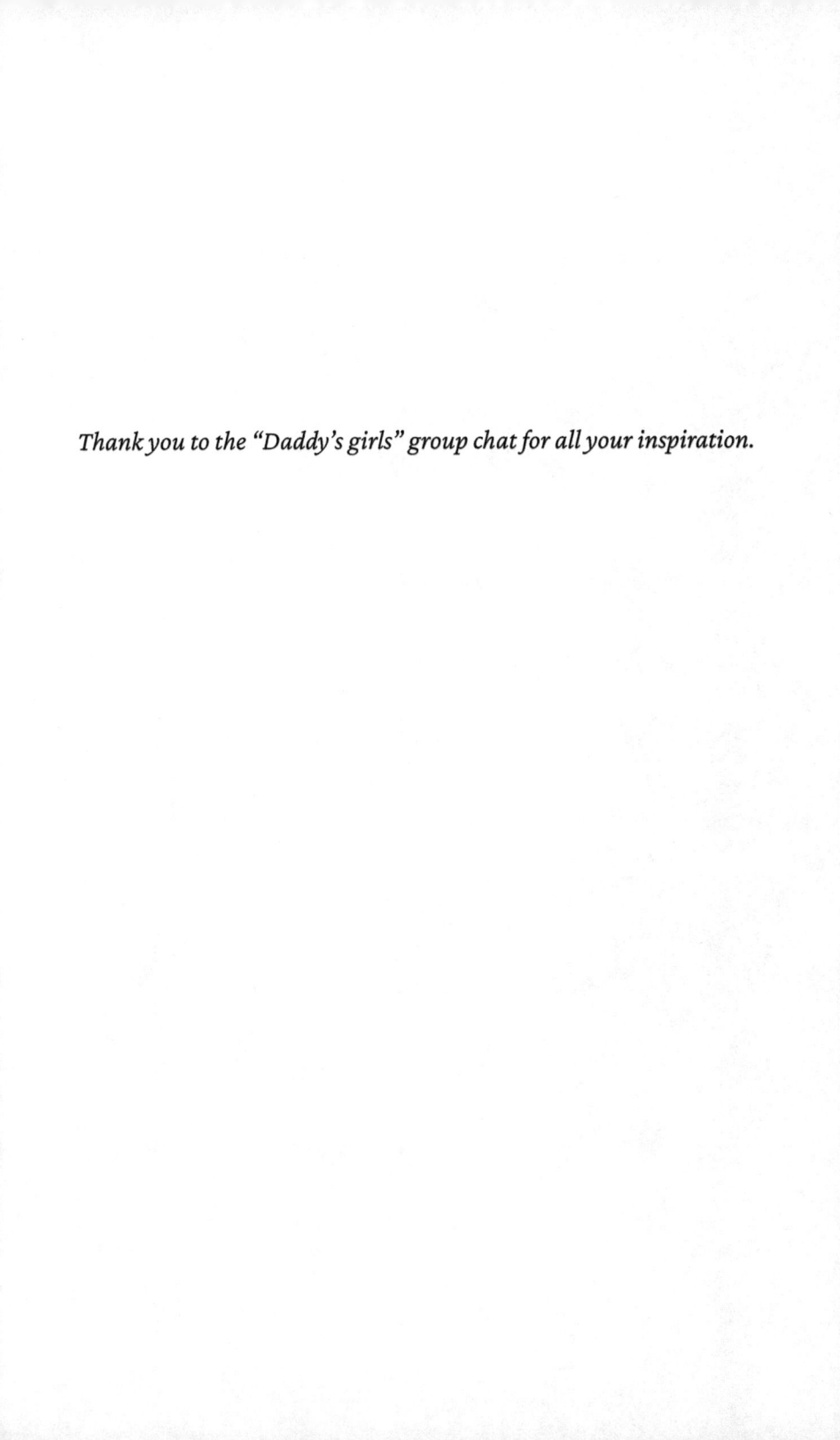

Thank you to the "Daddy's girls" group chat for all your inspiration.

CONTENT/TRIGGER WARNINGS

Alcohol/drug use
Purposeful drugging of FMC by MMC
Light bondage
Somnophilia
Graphic on page sexual scenes
Explicit language
Taboo Relationship

PLAYLIST

Grown Man Cry - EMELINE

It Wasn't Me - Carleigh

SLIDE - gone dark & Dre Tamashi

WATCH THIS - TAELA

Deep Dive - Zarayah

You Stupid Girl - Framing Hanley

LIPSTICK - gonedark & 47stillstanding

Dangerous - Sleep Token

Casual Sex - My Darkest Days

Touchin' Me - Chandler Leighton

False God - Taylor Swift

Dear God - Tate McRae

Forbidden Fruit - Rommee Profitt, Sam Tinnesz & Brooke

THE TEAMS

Girls Roster

    Lucy Simmons - Goalkeeper - #1

    Anja Sinclair - Right Fullback - #2

    Maeghen Rodriguez - Left Fullback - #3

    Chelsey Harrington - Center Back - #4

    Aaliyah Brooks - Center Back - #5

    Blake Aster - Striker - #6

    Isabelle Dubois - Defensive Midfielder - #7

    Mayson Dunne - Central Midfielder #8

    Amara Patel - Right Midfielder - #9

    Emily Carter - Attacking Midfielder - #10

    Samira (Sam) Oakley - Left Midfielder - #11

    Leila Haddad - Defender- #12

    Camila Torres - Midfielder - #14

    Thao Nguyen - Forward - #15

    Coach: Carmichael

Boys Roster

    Madsen (Mads) Keller - Goalkeeper - #1

Malik Johnson - Right Fullback - #2

Walker Bradford - Left Fullback - #3

Luca Marquez - Center Back - #4

Elias Reyes - Center Back - #5

Kenji Tanaka - Defensive Midfielder - #6

Chase Douglas - Right Midfielder - #7

Matteo Reynolds - Central Midfielder #8

Colin Masters - Striker - #9

Zayne O'Neill - Attacking Midfielder - #10

Dante Gomez - Left Midfielder - #11

Omar El-Sayed - Defender- #12

Ryan Walker - Midfielder - #14

Emory DeVito - Forward - #15

Jake Miller - Utility Player - #16

Coach: Doc

RED CARD RITES

In times of old... or at least since the days when men still believed themselves gods among mortals (so, roughly a decade ago), a ritual most foul took root in the hallowed grounds of Northgate University.

'Twas not a test of skill nor a trial of strength, but a rite of mischief and torment, passed down from one generation of miscreants to the next.

Each year, as the autumn leaves fall and the air grows crisp with the scent of battle (and overpriced pumpkin spice lattes), the senior warriors of the men's soccer team, drunk on power and the unearned confidence of their forebears, select a victim from the junior ranks of the women's team. A singular soul upon whom they shall unleash a campaign most merciless, for reasons lost to time (and probably testosterone).

The rules are thus:

1. Thy mark must be chosen at random. Those chosen must remain so until the very end. The feistier, the better, for the greatest entertainment is wrought from the greatest suffering. The only exemption lies in those bound by courtship, for none already claimed may be claimed again.

2. Break her spirit by means both cunning and calculated. Fill her locker with something truly vile—perhaps an assortment of questionable raw meats, carefully sourced for maximum horror. Let whispers spread through the kingdom that she hath forged secret alliances with the enemy, her loyalty now in question. Ensure she wakes in an unfamiliar location, relocated under the cover of darkness, not far enough to cause true panic, but just enough to ruin her morning. And, if the gods of mischief allow it, see that she enjoys a night of restless torment before the season's most critical match, alarms set at random, mysterious knocks upon her door, a well-timed playlist of unsettling noises. Victory favors the most relentless.

3. Deny all, lest ye be weak. Should suspicion fall upon thee, feign innocence, shed tears if thou must, and cast blame upon a brother-in-arms. Loyalty means naught in this war.

But lo, the women's team hath never been content to suffer in silence. Nay, with fire in their hearts and vengeance upon their tongues, they have turned the tide in years past. The mighty have been felled by ruined reputations, keys that vanish ere dawn's first light, and lockers that house not gear, but swarms of ravenous insects.

And yet, the air crackles with unspoken tension, the calm before the inevitable storm. The season has begun, the battle lines are drawn, and soon—very soon—The Selection will be upon us.

PROLOGUE

COLIN

Every year, the older guys on the team participate in the Red Card Rites and we've just had to watch. This is finally our year. The start of soccer season signals the beginning and I finally get to drive her crazy.

Sure, I've fucked with her over the years, and she hates me, which is exactly what I've wanted. Especially considering it's all lead up to this. No one can tell me no because Mayson is mine. She's been mine since the day she walked into my house as my new stepsister. She's going to continue to be mine. Mine to fuck with, mine to torment, mine to conquer.

"Alright everyone, time to pick names," our captain, Mads Keller, announces. His British accent seems to get more pronounced when he gets louder.

I'm leaning against the lockers, but as he pulls out the mesh bag with the folded papers of names on the girls' team, I kick off them, and stand up on a bench. I don't need to raise my voice to get the attention of my teammates, they're going to listen to me regardless.

"I get Mayson." My tone holds no room for arguments.

1

"That's not how it works, Masters," my teammate, Elias Reyes, murmurs.

"It is when she's mine and none of you fuckers get to mess with her except me, got it?"

"Sit down," Keller demands.

I jump off the bench, but don't sit, just go back to leaning against the lockers. "You pull Mayson, you hand her over."

"Or what?" Lucas Marquez, another one of my teammates, snickers.

"Or I'll fucking kill you." I glare at him.

"For fucks sake." Keller pulls out his selection then passes the bag around for everyone else to do the same.

I watch their faces, keeping my arms folded across my chest. I don't even touch the bag when it gets to me, and watch as it moves onto the next person. Chase Douglas's eyes go wide when he unfolds his paper and his eyes shoot up to me. I put my hand out. "Give it."

He does so without argument. I snatch the paper immediately, looking down and seeing her name.

I smirk. Mayson Dunne, it's time to play.

CHAPTER 1
MAYSON

I remember the day my mom told me our life was going to change. I knew she'd been dating this guy for a few months, though she wouldn't tell me much about him. Turns out our life was changing because that man was super fucking rich. And she was going to marry him. At fifteen, right before my sophomore year, I was uprooted, moved into her future husband's new mansion on Mercer Island and was forced to attend some richy-rich high school.

The worst part came when I met *him*. My new stepbrother, Colin.

A door slams from somewhere inside the house, and I hear my mother call my name, "Mayson, come say hi."

I really don't want to say hi to whoever this is. I've been paraded around all summer by my mom and her soon to be husband. I'm sick of it. Their wedding is in two days and the past few weeks have been filled with appointments, tasting, meetings, and family none of us care about. The last thing I want right now is to meet another person.

She calls out for me again, so I drag myself from my new bed, which is way nicer than the one I had in our old apartment, and go downstairs.

That's when I see him, well the back of him. He's tall with broad shoulders, and his T-shirt is so tight I can practically see the muscles on his back. He has a backward baseball cap on, but the ends of his dark hair stick out from underneath it.

"*Mayson, this is my son, Colin,*" *Walter, my mom's fiancé, introduces.*

Colin turns around, his eyes are blue, but not like any blue I've ever seen, they are darker. They remind me of the ocean. Those same eyes look me up and down, then he opens his mouth to speak, but all he says is, "*That's it?*"

My jaw drops. No hi, no nice to meet you, nothing, just "*that's it?*"

I fold my arms across my chest, "*Well I don't know what you were expecting asshole, but yeah,* that's it."

"*Mayson!*" *my mom scolds.*

Colin smirks. "*Welcome to the family, sis.*"

"*I'm not your fucking sister.*"

"*Mayson Anne!*" *Mom screeches using my middle name. I hate when she does that.*

Colin steps closer to me, and I grimace. "*Not yet, but in two days you will be.*"

Those two days came and went, and so did even more torment from him.

I'm busy collecting the bouquets from the side room they were put in which caused one of mom's many meltdowns for the day. Apparently they were supposed to be in the bridal suite, waiting for her when we arrived. They weren't and now here I am trying to juggle seven bouquets. Yes, seven. I didn't know she had six friends, I figured her bridesmaids would be me, and maybe one other person. But somehow she has all these new prissy friends.

The door clicks shut, and I spin around quickly, balancing some of the flowers in my arms. I'm met with that same dark blue stare from the last person I want to see right now.

I'd hoped to keep my distance from him. I thought he would be with his dad the whole day, but that's obviously not the case.

"What do you want?" I snap.

He raises his hands up. "Just checking to see if you needed any help."

I narrow my eyes at him. "I don't believe you."

He smirks. "You shouldn't."

"Get out of my way," I demand.

"Nah, I want to make a few things clear." He kicks his foot back, leaning against the door, blocking my exit. "Just because you're moving into my house, coming to my school, and invading my life, doesn't mean you belong in it."

"You act like I want any of this, trust me it's the last—"

"I wasn't done," he cuts me off and I'm tempted to throw some of these flowers at his face. "If you see anything I do, you don't snitch to our parents. You don't talk to any of my teammates. And don't get a crush on me."

I scoff and roll my eyes. "I don't give a shit what you do or don't do. I don't care to know any of your stupid teammates and I would never like you."

Mom told me he plays soccer, and she thought it was something we could bond over since I've played my entire life. There's no bonding to be had, and I've tried telling her that, but she doesn't care.

"We'll see about that." He moves out of the way to open the door again, stepping out first. I turn back to try and grab all the flowers because I refuse to ask him for help. I hear him speak one more time and grind my teeth to fight my reply. "You're not special just because your mom is marrying my dad. You're still a nobody and always will be."

I thought after the wedding and once school started Colin

would want to avoid me at all costs. He wants me to leave him alone, he would do the same for me. That was not the case, and even though he's a year older than me, he was around a lot more than I would have liked both at school and at home.

It's like he wanted to find reasons to get pissed at me. He set the ground rules, and then made it impossible to follow them. He wanted me to know he's the one in charge, but I'll never go down without a fight. Not then and not now.

We unfortunately ended up at the same college because of the elite soccer program Northgate has for both men and women. My mom was glad my "brother" would be there to look out for me when I went away. Little does she know the only one I need looking out from is him.

Especially now.

It's the start of Red Card Rites; we're all warned about it before our Junior year, we all witnessed it our earlier years here. Now it's our turn. We don't know when the torment begins, but we know it's coming.

We also don't know who picks us, but I do. This is war and it's a long time coming. I know neither of us are going to hold back.

"Hey Mace, are you coming out with us?" my teammate and roommate, Blake asks.

"Obviously."

If Colin thinks I'm going to stay home and hide he's sorely mistaken. I'm going to push him to his limits and I'm going to have fun doing it.

CHAPTER 2
COLIN

My dad bought a townhouse near campus for me to live in while I attend Northgate. It's just off campus, and perfect for parties. It ended up becoming the unofficial team hang out spot. Which is fine with me until I want some privacy. Then I kick all the fuckers out to have the place to myself, and usually whatever girl I choose.

When Mayson announced she was going to attend Northgate, both my dad and her mom suggested she move into the townhouse with me.

"You won't have to worry about having some weird roommate. It's perfect," her mom suggests.

I'm sitting on the couch, my leg crossed over my knee, and smirking at Mayson's pissed off face. "Yeah, you just have me."

"I'd rather go swim with sharks." She grimaces.

I laugh. "Aw, I don't bite as hard as a shark. Unless you want me to."

"Colin, enough," my dad snarls and I roll my eyes. He knows he has no control over me, though he likes to pretend he does in front of his new little family.

I lived with my mom until dear old dad insisted I move in with him my Junior year of high school. He was getting married and wanted to have a family again. Mom never cared much whether I was home or not, so she had no problem shipping me back to him.

And then I saw Mayson and I knew I wasn't going to fight it.

"I'd rather get the whole college experience, dorms and all that," Mayson insists and I don't hide my scoff. No one actually wants to live in the dorms, but I know she just wants to be away from me.

Too bad she never will be, despite what she thinks. I've made sure she knows I'm still around, even as I've been at college, not that Northgate is far. I know she knows it. None of the guys will talk to her, and those that dare to try learn really quickly why they shouldn't.

"Fine. But if there's even the slightest problem, you're moving in with Colin," her mom states.

I'm unable to hide the way the corner of my mouth curls up at that. I'll remember that threat, especially because I know she'll hate it.

I'll let her have her freedom for a bit. At least I'll let her think she does. Everything she does is only because I let her, and she's going to learn that sooner rather than later.

"That's settled, then. Colin," my dad looks at me, "Take care of your sister while you're there."

"Not your fucking sister," I hear her grumble while I smile widely.

"Don't worry, I'll make sure she's well taken care of."

And I will. In my own way.

The Rites begin at midnight, and the first order of business is about to begin. I need to get her close to me. She's not going to like it, and that makes it even better for me.

But tonight the team is hanging out, drinking, and of course even when I don't intend for it to turn into a party it always does. It doesn't take long for the girls on Mayson's team to start showing up like they usually do. Though, she rarely does. On the rare occasions she does come, she makes it a point to ignore me completely.

Tonight she has no choice, and as soon as midnight hits she's not leaving.

I'm nursing a beer that's gone warm in my hand. I have to force it down because there's not much worse than warm beer. I'm on high alert for Mayson, but haven't seen her. I know she's coming; I recognize almost everyone else on her team except I don't see her.

"Hey Colin," a woman's voice says next to me as I feel a hand around my bicep.

I look down to see who it is, and don't even bother to hide my grimace. She's not the girl I need the attention of tonight. I'm pretty sure I've hooked up with her before, she's not on the woman's team, and I couldn't tell you her name for the life of me.

"Not interested," I grumble.

"Aw, you sure? You don't even have to do anything." She runs her tongue along her bottom lip, and I wait to see if my dick reacts at all, but there's nothing. Nada.

"Yeah, I'm sure." I look around once again, and don't miss the pouty look she gives me before stomping away.

I storm over to the first teammate I see. "Reyes," I snap. "You seen Mayson?"

He shakes his head and I scowl, walking away before he gets the chance to say anything because I worry if anyone dares to speak a few words to me before I see Mayson they may end up on the ground. I'd rather not have to explain to our coaches why I beat up someone.

Again.

I finish off my drink, tossing it in one of the waste bins and refuse to reach for another one just yet. Another girl tries to get my attention, but I shake her off. Tonight is one of the first times I'm annoyed by the attention I get because I'm too focused.

Then I see her. She's in between two other girls I'm sure are on her team, but I couldn't tell you their names. I don't really care to know them anyway. My large strides bring me over to her quickly, and the second she notices her eyes narrow.

"How nice of you to grace us with your presence," I taunt.

"Ew, I forgot this is your house," she lies.

"It's your house too, since we're family and all."

"We are not family."

Don't I know it. If she was my family I wouldn't have the thoughts about what I would do to her body. How I would fuck her awake, fill her with so much of my cum she would feel me leaking from her little pussy for days.

No, we aren't family.

But it pisses her off when I make comments like that. Which is why I'll never stop.

"Have fun." I stretch my arm out to let her walk past me. Mayson gives me a disbelieving look.

One of her friends mumbles, "Let's go," and pulls the other two deeper into the house.

I stop Mayson with a hand on her bicep, dropping my lips to her ear. "Not too much fun."

"You don't tell me what the fuck to do."

"You sure about that?" I let go of her, and back away.

She keeps her eyes trained on me, clearly waiting for more. But she's safe for a couple more hours. I really will let her have some fun, I'll just be watching and figuring out how much worse I'm going to make her life as soon as it turns midnight.

CHAPTER 3
MAYSON

"That was fucking weird," my teammate Anja murmurs.

"Not really, that's just Colin."

I feel his eyes on me throughout the night, and I'm just waiting for him to pounce. I'm trying not to drink too much because I have to stay alert around him. But when the drinks start to hit me a little harder than I expect, I wonder if I didn't eat enough.

I can't even remember what I ate today.

The room is spinning.

Where did my friends go? I swear I was staying next to them and they wouldn't just leave me.

God, my head feels horrible; I swear I didn't drink that much. I don't think I've ever felt this drunk before in my entire life. This is awful.

I lose my balance because suddenly I feel like my legs don't work. My instant thought is that I'm not going to be able to play soccer anymore if I can't use my legs.

"You'll be able to play soccer," a deep voice says, and I didn't even realize I spoke.

I recognize the stupid voice as Colin, but he sounds so far away. My vision is so blurry I can hardly make out his stupid attractive face. I hate that he's good looking because it would make hating him a lot easier if my body got on board. Instead, physically I want him when the rest of me wants to punch him in the face.

"I knew you thought I was hot," he says with a laugh.

I can't believe I said that out loud as well, I'm just going to clamp my mouth shut. I try to do just that, but he laughs again, and I swear I'm being taken somewhere. I can't ask where because my mouth is shut and I don't know how to unstick my lips together.

My back hits a bed, and the room around me continues to spin. I'm able to open my mouth again because a tiny piece of self preservation finally kicks in. I'm unable to form any words so I just start to scream.

A hand clamps over my mouth and I try to thrash, but my entire body feels heavy and weak. I can barely even lift my arm to hit the dark figure looming over me. I don't even get to make contact with any part of him before my limb falls onto the bed.

"No one is going to come save you, but don't worry I'm not going to hurt you," Colin pauses before adding, "yet."

I squeak out a protest that gets lost behind his heavy hand over my mouth, while my head spins.

"Welcome to Hell. I've been waiting for you to join me." He threatens darkly.

His hand slips away from my mouth, and his body moves further away. I'm unable to move, speak, or do anything. I think I see some light as he exits the room, but I'm passed out before he even shuts the door behind him.

WHEN I WAKE up I have the hangover from hell. This isn't like anything I've ever felt before. My head is pounding and even the small amount of light shining into the unfamiliar room has me slamming my eyes shut once again. A groan tries to escape my throat, but it feels like I swallowed a bunch of knives. My entire body feels heavy, but at least I'm able to move, kind of.

As I'm trying to get myself oriented, a loud banging starts and it only gets closer. The door swings open, and Colin is hitting a pan with a wooden spoon. I cover my ears from the piercing sound, wanting to scream, but I feel like my throat will actually slice open if I do.

"Get up, sleepyhead!" he yells, and then continues the banging.

"Fucking stop!" I finally manage to yell, and crack my eyes open a bit more to see he's standing there with that stupid smirk on his face.

Oh god, he's shirtless, revealing his tanned, toned chest from the constant work outs. His basketball shorts hang low on his hips and that single silver chain he wears is dangling around his neck.

"Don't worry, babe, you'll get lots of time to ogle me now that you live here, but you gotta get up." He leaves before I have time to process what he just said.

When it finally hits me, I'm rushing out of the bed I was in, tripping over the sheets. I do my best to ignore the way my head feels like it's going to cave in on itself as I chase after him.

Colin is in the kitchen, shaking up his protein shake like he does every morning. I am always fascinated by the way his arm muscles bulge, and how the veins pop under his skin. He flicks the lid open, and takes a big swig from the drink, his eyes on me, and an eyebrow raised.

I fold my arms across my chest, which is when I notice I'm not in the clothes I was wearing last night. I'm in one of *his* soccer jerseys.

"What the fuck am I wearing?" I screech. "You undressed me?"

He just looks at me, the side of his mouth pulled up.

"Colin, I swear to fucking god. Why am I in your house and in your stupid jersey." I pluck the fabric away from my body like it's going to burn me. That's when I realize I'm only wearing underwear and my bra underneath it so my options right now are this or being practically naked in front of my stepbrother.

He leans on the counter separating us, and I can't help but stare at those stupid arms of his. Everything of his is stupid.

Hot, but stupid.

"You're in *our* house, and in my jersey."

I scoff, "This isn't our house. My mom said as long as I stayed out of trouble I got to stay on my own."

"Yeah, well that's over," he says, suddenly serious.

"I haven't done anything to get in trouble, what do you mean?"

He doesn't say anything, just pulls his phone out, and comes toward me, showing me his screen. "Press play."

I really don't want to because I'm worried about what I'm about to see. But the frozen image on the screen is very clearly me from last night, with Colin holding me up. I press play, and watch, horrified as my practically limp body is carried by him into another room.

"You were drugged last night, I'd say that's some trouble," he tells me seriously.

"Who the fuck drugged me?" I cry out, though it does make sense. I didn't think I drank that much, and even when I have been drunk, it's never felt like that.

He shrugs. "Doesn't matter, but what does is that the second I show this to dear old mom and dad, they're going to want you right here with me. I just beat them to it."

"You're not showing them."

"Aren't I? You have no say. Either I show them, and you move in here, or I don't show them, but you move in here."

I grumble about what an asshole he is.

"You can be pissed about it, but it's not going to change anything. Welcome home."

"Why are you doing this?"

"You know exactly why. I have to go work out. You better still be here when I get back, and if you're not I'm going to get you and bring you back."

"You can't make me."

"Watch me."

I'm WARMING up with my teammate Maeghen, kicking the ball back and forth while we wait for our drill to start.

"You good?" she asks, passing the ball back to me.

I stop it, kicking it up, bouncing it on the top of my foot, then onto my knee before letting it fall back onto the grass. "I fucking hate the stupid Red Card Rites." I kick the ball a little harder than necessary.

"Sh," she shushes me, looking around to make sure no one heard.

I roll my eyes, yeah the first rule of the Rites is to not talk about the Rites, or something like that. We don't actually know the rules because it's totally misogynistic and run by the guys while we're just supposed to take it. Well, fuck that.

"Colin thinks I'm going to move in with him just so I can be his hostage for whatever he has planned for me."

She grimaces. "Just don't move in then."

"Yeah, I have a feeling he's not exactly going to give me an option."

I leave out the part about me being drugged last night because I don't need to be spreading that around campus and getting everyone worried. Plus, if it came back that it happened at Colin's, I'm sure there would be even more issues and he would know it was me that told.

It's like I can't win in anything other than soccer lately.

"Anything happen to you lately?" I ask, passing the ball back.

She shakes her head. "Doesn't mean I'm in the clear, though."

It's true, not everyone gets picked because the guys have the option to opt out, but usually only if they're in a serious relationship. Though, I'm not sure how many of the guys actually choose not to participate. This is basically considered the men's team World Cup of Northgate.

"Alright, ladies, line up," Coach Carmichael calls out.

After practice we're all in the locker room changing and I overhear some of the girls talking about what the guys have done so far. Petty, stupid things, but I know it's only going to escalate. It always does. Every year we hear and see what happens.

Then there's Halloween.

I know one thing and it's that I'm not going to take any of this lying down. I'm going to fight back. Whether it's Colin or not, since he's so hellbent on making my life miserable, especially now, he's going to have to deal with me serving it right back.

Something tells me my teammates are all going to agree that it's time to turn the tables. The guys aren't the only ones that get to have the fun.

CHAPTER 4
COLIN

I know Mayson's schedule probably better than I know my own. I need to make sure she's where she's supposed to be because if not then she could be somewhere or with someone she shouldn't be. Am I overprotective? Not exactly. I just don't want her having too much fun.

Especially not with someone she shouldn't be.

Like fucking any of the guys around here.

It was the same thing when she was in high school. I made sure no one touched her. She's still a virgin as far as I know, and she fucking better be. Now with her under my roof again, there's no way that's changing for her with anyone other than me.

It was always going to be me.

Doesn't matter if people think it's wrong, she's mine to own in every single way, including her body. I'm going to be her one and only. Her pussy will only know my cock and that's the way it should be.

But not yet. She's going to crave it, crave me even more than she already does even though she won't admit it. I'm

17

going to drive her crazy first. It's the Rites, after all, and she's my target. I'll push her to her breaking point and then I'll take her all for myself.

I finish up with my workout and practice, getting home before her. I know she takes her time after practice. She's always taken long showers, I can only imagine how thorough she is washing her long dark hair. The way the water falls over her body, as she slides her hands through it, washing herself.

One day it'll be my hands, grabbing that same skin and my tongue tracing the trail the water leaves over her.

Soon.

I also know she's going to try and go home first, that's when she's going to see that I've taken the liberty to move all her stuff for her. I'm generous like that.

I'm sitting on my couch, feet kicked up and scrolling through my phone while I wait. Of course I have her location shared so I'm able to check in periodically, which is why I know exactly when she gets to her *old* home.

Now, it's only a matter of time before she shows up here. I should've set up cameras in her room to see her reaction. Dammit, I should've thought that through a bit more. *Next time.*

My front door is thrown open so hard it hits the wall, and without looking I know it's a pissed off brunette.

"Colin what the *fuck?*" Mayson screeches, and I'm unable to hide my self satisfied smirk.

"I told you, babe, you live here now."

"Stop calling me that you asshole. What the fuck did you do?"

"You clearly aren't safe, I talked to the RA of your dorm then nicely moved your shit out for you. You're welcome."

I paid for it to be moved, but semantics.

"Did you tell my mom? Or your dad?"

"I let them know you'd be living here," I grunt. Because no, I'm not about to tell them the details. Even if I was the one that slipped the drug into her drink, it wasn't to hurt or take advantage of her. I want her fully aware when I do that. It was just to get the ball rolling.

She narrows her eyes and I meet her glare with my own.

Then something happens I didn't expect. Her face softens, and she shrugs her shoulders. "Okay."

Okay?

She walks past me toward the stairs and I just watch her go, waiting for her to retaliate. To scream at me, maybe try to hit me or something. All the things she's normally done. But she doesn't.

She just walks away. I don't even hear the bedroom door slam. I'm frozen while I wait for a scream, a crash, some sort of retaliation, but there's just...nothing.

I don't like it. I want the reaction from her, that's the fun of it all. Though, she's surprised me before. Just like the time I fucked her best friend when I knew she would be coming home. She didn't know I was back from break my freshman year while she was still in her senior year of high school. I didn't give a fuck about her friend, I just knew she'd tried to sit on my dick for years.

Mayson was at practice or a game or some shit and I made sure she'd come home to see her friend riding me. She stood there completely frozen. I expected her to scream or react in some way, but she didn't. I looked directly into Mayson's wide eyes while her friend screamed faker than a porn star, and I winked.

She took off into the house and I got rid of her friend as fast as possible. The next day I went to get dressed and realized my stepsister had cut a hole in every single one of my shorts. Right where my dick lays.

I couldn't even be mad, I was just impressed.

Of course, she's also a fighter and there's been plenty of times she's reacted instantly with screaming, and throwing fists at me.

I push off the couch because I'd rather not give her the opportunity to cut holes in more of my shit again. When I get upstairs I notice her door, which is right next to mine, is closed, and that mine is exactly how I left it.

I'm not sure if I should be relieved or worried. Turns out I'm neither. I'm excited, and hard as a rock thinking about her being so close to me again. Just like when we were younger. I couldn't do anything about it then. Couldn't have our parents finding out, but now they aren't around.

No one is here to stop me from doing anything I want to her, and that's exactly what I intend to do.

Entering my room, I don't shut the door before laying on my bed. I think about how close she is. I think about everything I have planned for her. My cock throbs behind my shorts, so I push them down, wrapping my fist around my hard length. I don't muffle or hold back the groan I let out at the feeling of my hand tightening around myself.

I don't even feel the need to pull my phone out to put on some porn, just knowing Mayson is close enough to hear me, that she could walk by any second and watch, is enough. I remove my hand for just a second to spit into my palm before gripping myself once again and moving my fist rapidly.

I think about it being Mayson's pussy, her mouth or her ass. *Fuck,* I know any part of her will feel like heaven. And knowing my dick will be the first has me moving my hand even harder over myself. I'm not going to last long because I know exactly what I need and this is purely about release.

This is because I want her to hear me. I want her to *want* to come in here and clean up the cum I get all over my hand.

"Fuck, Mayson, you're going to feel so fucking good," I groan, imagining the way she would bend over on my bed, pushing her ass up for me, looking back with that evil little glint in her eye. The one that challenges me and makes me want to force her into submission for me.

"Yeah, you're going to take it. I'm going to fill you so fucking full and watch my cum drip out of you," I groan at the visual. I'm unable to hold back as my release barrels toward me, my balls draw up, and ropes of cum shoot out onto my stomach.

Looking down at the mess on my abs, I glance at the doorway, and there she is. Eyes wide, looking at me just like that day she saw me fucking her friend.

She doesn't move, even when I stand up, tucking my softening dick away and walk toward her. Her eyes don't leave mine. When I'm finally in front of her, looking down at her face, I taunt, "Either get down and clean me up, or go back to your room."

That breaks her out of the trance she was in, scoffing and shaking her head, but she doesn't move.

I step backwards, raising my eyebrow. She looks down at my stomach, then back up and when she goes to open her mouth, I don't let her say whatever it is she's about to because I'm shutting the door right in her face.

It's not time yet. She's not broken enough, but she will be.

CHAPTER 5
MAYSON

That stupid son of a bitch. I stomp back to what I guess is now considered my room in this stupid house. After seeing Colin's stupid face and catching him jerking off his stupid dick I didn't know what to do. I still don't. He slammed the door in my face, and it's probably for the best because I don't know what I would have done. Probably something stupid that I shouldn't have. Everything is just *stupid*.

But he took the chance away and I'm distracting myself going through my things he had moved over here. It doesn't take very long for me to realize that a bunch of my clothes are missing.

Like the majority of them.

I have one T-shirt, one pair of pants, one light jacket, one pair of socks, one uniform, and no panties.

I look through all the drawers in the single dresser, and don't find anything else. Everything else of mine is here, even the bedding on the bed is from my old room. My computer, books, even random papers are sitting on the desk almost exactly how I left them.

The only thing missing is my clothes.

I storm back to Colin's room, and pound on his door, my anger replacing any of the horniness he caused. When the door swings open he's still shirtless, with just that single silver chain he always wears around his neck and the loose shorts on his waist. He leans against the door frame.

"Need something?" he questions, with a slight upturn of his lip.

"Uh yeah, my clothes. Where are they?"

"Noticed that, huh?"

"No shit. What did you do with them? I need more than just one uniform."

"You can wear mine." His self satisfied smirk appears again and I roll my eyes.

"I can't wear *your* uniform to *my* games you idiot."

"You can for practice." He pauses. "And you can work on earning your clothes back."

I fold my arms across my chest. "Yeah? How are you wanting me to do that? Sucking your dick or something?"

His hand slaps against his chest like he's shocked. "Of course not, what kind of brother would that make me?"

"The disgusting kind, which is exactly what you are."

"Now that's not very nice," he scolds. "I'll let this one go for now, but you can earn your clothes back doing things around here for me."

"Like a fucking maid? You have one of those." I roll my eyes. He *would* want something like that from me. That's when I get a glimmer of an idea. One of the ways I can fuck with him. He wants me to be his slave? I'll make sure to torture him right back.

"I fired her." He shrugs.

I smile widely, the fakest over the top smile I can manage. "Fine. I cook, clean, and get my clothes back?"

"Yeah, we'll start there and see how you do." He steps closer to me, I keep my eyes on his, refusing to back down and show any weakness. "But you're going to do what I say."

"We'll see about that."

This time, I'm the one that walks away first. I expect him to grab me, but he lets me leave. Which is good because I close myself in my room again and stop myself from screaming into a pillow. I have to stay strong. I have to be the one that wins.

IT'S BEEN A FEW DAYS, and Colin is supposed to have some of his team over to hang out. He seems to do this a lot, there was a bonfire my first official night I lived here. I avoided that like the plague. This time he told me to stay away, the same way he used to in high school, never wanting anyone on his team to give me any attention.

But we aren't in high school anymore, and we're in a battle.

I'm wearing a large T-shirt and that's it. He took my panties, and hasn't given me any back so really this is his fault. I'm cooking myself dinner, just waiting for Colin and his friends to get here. I refuse to go hide, at least not before I fuck with him a bit.

I'm even baking some cookies. I'm sure they are going to be devoured by the men coming here unless I hide them in my room, which I just might. They're snickerdoodles, my favorite, so I may have to.

The front door opens and I hear the loud voices of the four guys entering. I turn around, leaning on the counter. Colin enters first and as soon as he sees me his eyes narrow.

"What're you doing?"

"Cooking, since I apparently live here, right? Isn't this what I'm supposed to be doing?" I taunt.

"Not today. I told you to not be around."

"Aw, come on Masters, your sis can hang around," one of the guys chimes in.

"Yeah, we could use something nice to look at," another one adds.

I smile flirtatiously and Colin immediately shuts it down, shoving his teammates away. They all laugh as they go to the living room and start up some video game. Colin keeps his narrowed eyes on me.

"What do you think you're doing?" he asks.

I shrug just as the oven timer goes off. I smirk, turning around, and making sure when I bend over, I do so slowly. I know that my shirt is riding up to show part of my ass and probably some of my pussy.

When I stand up I feel him right there, pushing me against the warm oven and I gasp. Especially as I feel his hard length pressing into me. I fight the urge to arch back against him.

"I know what you're fucking doing, and if any of them saw what you just did, I would have to gouge their eyes out for getting a glimpse of this perky little ass and that pink pussy. So you better think about that before you try to put on another show."

I turn my head, our lips closer than I thought, so close it wouldn't take much to close the distance between them. "Quite the threat, I can't wait to hear what you'll say when you catch me fucking one of them."

His hand shoots up, wrapping around the front of my throat, and bringing my entire body flush with his. I try to gasp but it's hard through the pressure he's got on my neck, and I bring my hands up to dig my nails into his arm.

"None of them will ever fucking touch you. I know you're

still a virgin, and if you think any of them deserve to be the one to change that, you are seriously mistaken."

He's right, I *am* still a virgin. I fucking hate that about myself, but no guy I've wanted has ever been the one to change that. I'm sure Colin is partly to blame for it, though I don't have proof. Or know *why* other than he likes to torture me.

But I don't want to give him the satisfaction of *knowing* he's right.

"What makes you think I'm still a virgin?"

He squeezes my neck tighter and I desperately try to suck in some air, but can't and I'm starting to panic. He wouldn't kill me, there're witnesses, but there's a moment I'm left wondering, *would he?*

"I know you are, and I'll be proven right when I have your blood smeared on my cock after I fuck this pussy full of my cum."

He lets me go, and I suck in deeply, savoring the air as my lungs fill with it.

"You'll never get the chance," I say, my voice weak.

He just laughs, joining his friends in the living room, and I'm left to question the wetness between my thighs. That shouldn't have turned me on and yet all I want to do is jump on him to relieve the ache he caused. *I must be seriously fucking deranged.*

Looking down at the fresh cookies, I smirk because I've never been someone to let things go. His threats don't scare me, I can handle anything he dishes out. I put the sweet treats on a plate, setting a couple aside for myself. Then, I steel my spine and walk into the living room, swaying my hips a bit more than I normally would.

Colin is in one of the chairs while two of his friends are manspread on the couch, and the other two are sitting on the floor for some reason. I step in front of Colin, bending over to set the plate of cookies on the coffee table.

"Thought you guys might like these," I say with the sweetest fake voice I can manage.

"Oh fuck yeah," one of them grunts, while they all immediately lean forward to massacre the cookies.

Two firm hands grab my hips, and yank me back onto a lap and I yelp in surprise. Colin wraps his arms around my middle, squeezing so hard I try to push him off me, but it's futile because he's extremely strong. Soccer players have strong legs, it's our prime tool for the sport, and especially a striker like Colin. But he makes sure to work out his upper body just as much which is evident by the defined muscles and the iron grip he has on me.

"What the fuck did I tell you?" he growls against my ear.

"When the fuck did I tell you I cared?"

He loosens his grip enough that I'm able to push away from him. I know this is just beginning, but damn does it feel good to fight back.

Now, if I could stop getting turned on when I feel his body close to mine, then that would be great.

CHAPTER 6

COLIN

I hardly pay attention in class because I know Mayson is back at my house, probably still sleeping. I made the mistake of peeking in on her before I left. I intended to see if she blocked her door, and when she didn't I took that as permission to enter. She may not be able to lock it, but she's creative.

She knows how to keep me out, if she doesn't do it then that's on her.

I saw her laying in bed, so peacefully her dark hair contrasting the white sheets. Her pink pouty lips tempted me to take them with my own, but I held back. I lifted the blanket to see what she's wearing since her clothing options are limited.

Thanks to me, of course.

Though, she's not getting her panties back no matter what she does.

Before I left her room I made sure to grab the one jersey I left her for soccer and replaced it with one of mine. For the past couple of days since her little stunt when my friends were over,

I let her think she was going to get away with it. I let her be comfortable and complaisant.

That's over.

I'm waiting for her to retaliate once she finds out what I did, which is another reason I can't pay attention. I can't tell you a single thing that was talked about in class, and I can't get out fast enough after the professor dismisses us.

I have a small break before my next class, then practice before I get to see Mayson again. She only has one class before her own practice and this weekend the girls have an away game. I don't like that she's going away. I've never cared as much before but now she's mine and I want to make sure she and everyone she comes into contact with, knows it.

I have my headphones in so I can ignore everyone as I grab a sandwich. Sometimes I don't care if people want to talk, but today I'm not in the mood. I stuff my face while walking to the building where my next class is and the hardcore music is pounding through my skull from the headphones.

Even as I sit down in class, I don't take my headphones out. I pull my phone out to check Mayson's location, and see she's on campus, from her speed it looks like she's walking. She's not that far from where I am. I think about getting up and skipping just so I can intercept her.

"Alright everyone, hope you're ready because we're going to go over your final projects." I inwardly groan. I'm sure I could get out of the stupid project, but I look down and see Mayson walked into another building and decide to leave her be.

She's safe for a couple more hours.

At practice we run through some drills and then start a scrimmage. I'm trying my best to keep my focus completely on the game, but when I hear her voice I think I'm imagining it. Then it gets louder, and my teammates notice it too, which means it's not just in my head.

"Colin!" Mayson calls out. I look over to see her pissed off. Her bottom half is in her shorts, shin guards and cleats ready to play. Her top half is only covered by a tight tank top. Her tits are pushed up at the top of it and I see red.

"Masters, deal with your shit another time," Doc, our coach, snaps, but I'm already halfway to where my pissed off stepsister is.

"I'll just be a second," I call back.

Mayson holds out the familiar jersey and I smirk, but even when I reach her I don't move to take it.

"Give me back my shit," she demands.

"I don't have it on me, feel free to try again later. And maybe try asking a bit nicer. I like the sweet ones."

"Eat a dick, Colin."

"I'd rather eat something else." My eyes trail down her body and my jaw clenches at the thought that my teammates are probably watching and seeing her perky little tits on display. "Cover up. You have a jersey, wear it."

"It's yours."

"Exactly. Put it on."

"No."

"Mayson, put the fucking jersey on or I won't give you anything back."

"So if I do then you'll return my clothes?" Her tone is hopeful.

I clench my jaw. "Try it and find out."

She hesitates and I see the way she battles with herself before reluctantly slipping the fabric over her head. "Happy?"

My tongue runs over my teeth before I let the smile take over. "Extremely."

Especially when she walks away and I'm able to see my name plastered across her back. I can't help but watch her ass move as she leaves to go to her own practice.

"Masters, if you don't get your ass back here I'm benching you."

Without saying anything, I jog back onto the field. If I were to open my mouth again I'm sure Doc would ream me even harder for what I say than she was already wanting to do. She's five-foot-two of intimidation. Except to me. I respect her as a coach, but she doesn't scare me like she does other guys on the team. They're either scared of her, or attracted to her. Or both. I'm neither.

"You're walking a fine line," Walker Bradford mumbles.

"Don't remember asking you," I retort.

Almost all of us are participating in the Rites, we all know how it goes. Some girls are feistier than others. I don't think any of us thought Mayson would go down easily, I like seeing her pissed off. I just don't like that my team also gets to see it.

Back when she was in high school, I remember threatening the entire boy's soccer team her senior year. If any of them thought they were going to have a chance with her just because I was at Northgate, they were going to learn just how wrong they were.

One tried. Fucking Jack Brolin. I went home unannounced like I did a lot that year and he was over for dinner. I glared at him the whole time, and finally got him outside where I made it very clear he wasn't welcome back in.

I waited until later that night to kick his ass, but I don't think Mayson knows about that.

If she does, she hasn't said anything to me about it. Which is not really usual for her, so I feel like she doesn't know.

After practice is over I skip on the shower because I plan to take one at home. With the door open, just in case my room-mate wants to take a peek. Or join me. Maybe I would let her just so I can put her in her place for the stunt she pulled today. And the other day. And anything else I'm sure she's planning.

I get home before her which I expected, so I take my time starting up the shower, getting undressed and into the hot water. I try to listen for the door as I lather the body wash on myself though it's not sudsing like it should. That's when I notice the smell is also different; I pause and then my skin starts to burn.

What the fuck?

I rinse off quickly, and when my skin is cleared, I notice it took the layer of hair off with it. I get out of the shower, wrap-ping a towel around my waist and storm over to the other bathroom. Without a care, I start ripping everything apart, searching for something—anything—and in the bottom drawer I find it. The bottle of hair remover. I open it to smell and confirm it, as soon as the cap is flipped the pungent smell hits me and I just shake my head.

It's a cute prank, a nice try. My intention is to destroy her. To break her down and then build her back up as only mine and this was nothing. Though it feels weird to have smooth skin, especially when I pull my clothes on.

I shake the feeling away and grab a beer from the fridge, sitting on the couch just waiting for her. The second the door handle turns, I don't even look, just bring the bottle to my lips, taking a sip and biding my time.

CHAPTER 7
MAYSON

I'm still pissed off and annoyed after practice. When I walk in the door, that feeling continues because I thought that maybe, just maybe, Colin would be out with his friends doing whatever the hell he wants. Instead, he's sitting on the couch drinking a beer. When I notice how shiny the arm lifting the bottle to his mouth is, I bite back a laugh.

I had the thought this morning, and I wasn't sure how long it would take, since I figured he showered at school. Guess I should've known better because Colin Masters is probably too good for locker room showers.

Part of me wants to make a smart ass comment about his smooth skin, the other part of me wants to continue avoiding him.

I choose to avoid conversation, walking past him without a word.

When I'm about to head upstairs he starts to speak.

"You have fun with your little prank?"

I bite back my smile, and don't turn around.

"It was cute, but I don't know why you think pulling something like that will get you your clothes back any sooner."

I snarl, turning back around toward him. "It doesn't matter because nothing I do will get you to give them back so you just want me to roll over and take it?"

He shakes his head. "No, I think I'd prefer you lay down and take it. Or maybe get on your knees. I'll have you doing all of it and more before long so I guess it doesn't really matter."

"You're disgusting"

"Yeah, you've said that, but we both know if I touched you that you wouldn't tell me to stop."

"You wouldn't even get close enough to touch me."

"No? Pretty sure I've had you in my lap already and if I'd slipped my fingers under the T-shirt you were wearing I would've been able to bury my fingers inside that needy cunt of yours. You wouldn't have had the chance to stop me."

My thighs clench, but I try to hide it.

"You wouldn't have done that in front of your teammates. Especially since you are *so* worried about them seeing an inch of my skin apparently."

His jaw tightens.

"They don't deserve to see any part of you, but if they were going to, it would only be while I'm claiming you so they can see what they can never have."

I shake my head, both trying to deny myself the way that he's making me feel and also trying to deny his words because I think he's actually gone insane. He's always made sexual jokes toward me, but I've always figured it was him just trying to get a rise out of me. Something about it now makes me feel like he may be serious.

Though he can't be. His dad is still married to my mom, and Colin is a certified fuck boy. Maybe he's just slept with every woman within a fifty mile radius except me and has decided that now it's time. I grimace at the thought.

"You don't like that idea, babe?" he teases. "Good because I don't either. They'll never get to see you like that."

"Neither will you."

He throws his head back on a laugh. "You're wrong about that."

I turn back around to walk up the stairs and continue to hear him laugh as I go. I'm sure he has more things planned for me. He's taken it relatively easy, but even I can feel that my time is limited. He's not one to let this go anytime soon.

COLIN RETURNED one of my jerseys. Just one, and I think it's because we have an away game that we leave for in the morning. There's no way he's just being nice, I bet he would prefer to keep the jersey away from me longer, but he's smarter than that.

I'm packing my away bag when I hear him come home. Other than the interaction we had after the hair removal incident, we haven't seen much of each other. Each day that goes by it makes me more and more uneasy. Then my jersey was laid on my bed, and he didn't say anything. He probably expected a thank you or for me to drop down to my knees praising his kindness.

If he expected that, then he should know he has the wrong bitch because I would never.

"I'm having a get together tonight," Colin states firmly from my doorway.

Get together is code for a party, just like it was in high school. I don't know why he's allergic to the word, but it's always been this way as long as I've known him.

"Congratulations," I deadpan.

"You're not invited."

"Too bad, I live here."

"Exactly, and you have a room you're going to stay in."

"You may think you're in charge, but you can't actually make me."

The side of his mouth lifts in a way that has a shiver running down my spine. "I can't?"

He looks around the room, that smirk still on his face, and when his eyes find mine again I know I should prepare to fight. That's especially true when he opens his mouth. "Enjoy your night, Mayson."

Before I can stop him he shuts the door, and I run over, immediately trying the handle but realize it's locked. From the outside. Because that asshole switched the door handle. I bang my fist against the wood. "Colin! You asshole, what's wrong with you?"

"Fuck, babe, I love the way you sound screaming my name. Can't wait to hear it when I'm inside you."

I scream in frustration, dropping onto the bed because I can't stand him. His footsteps hit the stairs, and I stare at the ceiling. If he thinks I'm just going to accept this he's *very* wrong.

He starts blasting his music downstairs, and I hate that we have a similar taste but it's not going to distract me. I finish packing my bag for the trip and then look in the mirror. My long dark hair is piled in a bun on top of my head and I'm in baggy clothes, not exactly party attire. But it's all I've been allowed by my captor. Since Colin is doing everything to make sure I don't go downstairs tonight, I'm going to do everything in my power to make sure I do.

⚽

THE VOICES GET LOUDER AS MORE people arrive. The music has changed to typical party music from the type Colin had playing earlier so I think someone else has taken over as the DJ. I wait until it gets later the night, even though I normally would be in bed because we leave early in the morning but I'm going to end up sleeping on the bus.

It'll be worth it to fuck with Colin.

I glance over to the mirror, taking in my appearance. My hair falls down my back in soft waves, and a light layer of makeup covers my face. I manage to improvise with my one pair of jeans and t-shirt I tie to show off a sliver of my stomach. Just like that, I'm ready to ruin my stepbrothers night.

My first thought is to attempt to break down the bedroom door, but that sounds like a lot of work. Instead, I step up to the one window, and look down into the side yard. It's sketchy, and if I fall I'll be fucked because I'm sure I'll end up breaking something, and I can't afford to not play soccer.

Some guy walks around the corner and lights up a cigarette, or a joint. Doesn't matter, he'll work.

I push open the window, leaning out and put in my best flirty expression. "Hey."

He looks around before finally looking up to see me, and I offer a smile with a little wave.

"Hi." He leans back, taking a drag from the rolled paper between his fingers. "What're you doing up there?"

"Super embarrassing," I lie. "I accidentally locked myself in my room." I pretend to play the damsel in distress, and the guy buys it easily.

"Oh man, I'll come up and help."

"No." I shake my head because I don't know where Colin is and I don't need him to catch this guy before I'm able to make it out of this room. "I can climb down, just make sure I don't fall," I tell him as sweetly as possible.

"Oh yeah, for sure." He puts out whatever he's smoking and acts like he's about to be my fucking savior or something even though I'm going to do all the work here. I just hope he won't let me fall and break my leg.

I glance around for my best course of action, trying to cause the least amount of damage possible to myself. Luckily, there's a ledge I think I can hold onto, and another one I might be able to reach and stand on if this guy can guide me down from there.

That's exactly what I do. My fingertips burn from the concrete as I climb down, but as soon as the toe of my Vans are firmly planted on the bottom ledge, I breathe out a small sight of relief.

His hands find my hips, and I can tell he's nervous about it which makes me roll my eyes. Luckily, he helps me down and my feet hit the ground with a thud. I smile up at the unfamiliar guy. "Thanks."

His eyes rove over my body, examining me and while he's attractive enough, he has nothing on Colin and the reminder just annoys me even more.

"What's your name?" he asks.

"Mayson," I answer, but don't even bother to ask for his.

"You need a drink after that?"

I smile, thinking about Colin seeing me with this guy. "Yeah, a drink sounds perfect."

CHAPTER 8
COLIN

Knowing Mayson is locked upstairs in her room probably fuming and planning my death has me in a better mood than usual. The woman currently grinding herself against my lap has absolutely nothing to do with it, though she may think differently. Especially because she's currently trying to fuck me through our pants, even though my dick isn't even hard.

The only person my dick is capable of getting hard for right now is my stepsister. The fact that she hates me only helps.

I swear my mind must be playing tricks on me since I can't stop thinking about her because I swear I see her entering the house from the backyard.

Grabbing the hip of the girl on my lap, I hold her down so she stops moving and obscuring my vision. Of course she thinks I'm doing it for other reasons and lets out a loud unnecessary moan, throwing her head back against my shoulder, turning so her lips graze my ear. "Want to go somewhere alone?"

My eyes are fixated on the woman across the room who I

know I'm not imagining when she turns to face some guy walking close behind her. I narrow my eyes, but she hasn't even looked in my direction. Instead, she's *smiling* to the asshole who now has his hand on her hip.

That small touch has me seeing red. Without a word, I toss whatever her name is off my lap, completely ignoring her shriek of frustration. I storm over to Mayson who's dancing with the guy who's wearing the most self-satisfied smirk and I'm about to drive my fist into his face.

Which is exactly what I do. It's a cheap shot, but I don't care.

Mayson gasps, pushing at my chest, "You fucking asshole, what's wrong with you?"

"Get out," I tell the guy currently holding his nose as blood pours from it. I didn't hit him hard enough to knock him to the ground, mostly because I don't need to cause more of a scene.

Though, everyone in here is watching, they won't say shit to Doc because they know it would only be worse if they snitched.

"Get out," I tell him again. I don't yell, I keep my voice deathly low because if he chooses not to listen, it's only going to get worse. For him, not me. He couldn't touch me.

"Colin, fuck off." Mayson pushes at my chest again, but I don't even spare a look at her. I'm watching the guy scramble and rush out of my house.

Once he's gone, I look down at the seething woman, who's beyond pissed at me, and I feel the same because she's not supposed to be down here. I glare at her, and without a word, grab her arm and pull her upstairs. The party hasn't paused for even a second, people are watching, but no one does anything to intervene, even as I roughly drag Mayson back up to her room while she tries to fight me off and screams. No one is coming to help her. They wouldn't dare get in my way.

She's trying to pry my fingers off her bicep as I unlock the door that's somehow still locked, and pull her into her room. I spin her around, pinning her against the door, by gripping her throat. Her hands shoot up to my wrist, digging her nails in as she glares at me. I tighten my grip enough to have her mouth dropping open as she gasps for air.

"What did I tell you?"

She opens her mouth but I squeeze even harder, cutting off her air so all she can do is gasp.

"Doesn't matter what I told you because you never fucking listen anyway."

Even though she can't take in a deep breath, her lip turns up in a small smirk, and I want to bite it away. I run my thumb up to pull her bottom lip down and she chases it with her teeth, barely nipping my skin.

I go back to squeezing her delicate little throat while she does her best to hide her gasps.

"Do you like driving me crazy?" I practically growl.

Her narrowed eyes are her only reply until I let up on my grip the smallest amount.

"I could say the same for you," she rasps.

I lean forward, bringing our faces so close together our lips are just a breath away from each other. "I'm only getting started."

I pull her mouth open with my thumb on her chin before bringing our mouths together, forcing my tongue past her lips while I seal my mouth over hers with a groan. She tries to fight me for just a second before letting her tongue tangle with mine as her hands fist my shirt.

It's hardly a kiss, more like a battle, one that I'm going to win. Because when it comes to her, I *will* win everything. Every battle, both for her body and in her life, is mine to fucking win. I tighten my grip around her throat again while deepening the kiss, and I feel the vibration of her moan against my palm.

I can't help my smile against her mouth. Especially when I take her bottom lip between my teeth and bite hard enough she yelps in surprise. I let go, soothing the sting with my tongue. I delve back into her mouth, licking and tasting every inch of her mouth I possibly can. Since right now she's actually letting me.

Though, I know that's not going to last much longer.

I take full advantage, pressing myself completely against her so she can feel how hard I am. I know she does by the gasp she lets out. I tighten my grip around her throat, kissing her viciously before pulling back.

Mayson's eyes are hazy as she looks up at me, but when it finally registers that I'm *me,* they harden and she clenches her jaw while trying to push me away.

I let go and allow her to push me away from her with a chuckle.

"What the fuck was that?" she screeches.

"A kiss, ever had one before?"

She's across the room, but turns to face me with her hands on her hips and fire in her eyes. It only makes me want to grab her and pull her underneath me on her bed, so I can fuck her into next week. But not yet.

"Yes, I have. I've done a lot more than you think," she sasses, and instantly my eyes narrow. I storm back over to her, crowding her against her desk, caging her in with my hands on either side of her hips.

"Tell me, what have you done?" I challenge.

She lifts her chin up, her brown eyes searing into me, burning with so much hatred and desire. It makes me want to take what's left of her virginity right here on this desk.

"Wouldn't you like to know."

"Yeah, actually I would," I push, trailing my finger down her jaw, onto her neck, to her shoulder, moving lower. "Has some asshole touched you here?" I graze over her bra covered chest.

"Maybe," she taunts.

A rumble sounds from the back of my throat, not liking her answer. But I continue, moving lower to her waistband and down to cup her over her shorts.

"And what about here?"

She smirks. I can see how she's going to answer before she even opens that pouty little mouth of hers. "What if someone has?"

"Then you're going to tell me who..." I grip her even tighter and she tenses. "And I'll kill him."

"You're not as tough as you think you are." She raises her chin up at me.

I hum, moving from cupping her pussy to her hand and guiding it to my erection. She gasps and tries to pull away, but I don't let her, holding her hand tightly against me.

"Have you touched anyone like this?" The anger is obvious in my voice and with the way I'm gripping her hand to squeeze me. It makes me want to push her hand inside my pants to feel how tightly she would wrap around me. How she would pump and fuck me with her soft hand.

"I've done more than that."

I grip her throat with my free hand again, tilting her head back, and pulling her bottom lip that's swollen from my teeth down.

"Have you had another man's cock in this bitchy little mouth?"

Her tongue peeks out and licks the tip of my thumb. It makes me tighten her hand around my cock even more. But she doesn't answer me, and it only makes me want to force the answer from her.

"Mayson," I threaten.

"Hm?"

"Have you sucked a cock before?"

"Doesn't matter if I have because I'll *never* suck yours."

I lean closer to her face again. "You also believed you'd never kiss me, and now I know what your mouth tastes like."

She squeezes my dick hard enough that I grunt. She leans closer to my face, mischief written all over hers. "Well, guess what? I *have* had another guys dick in my mouth. I *have* felt him in my hand and I *have* had *his* cum mark my skin. And there's not a damn thing you can do about it."

She knows exactly what she's doing, whether she's lying or not it doesn't matter. I grab her, tossing her onto the bed and straddle her hips, pinning her hands by the side of her head. She tries to buck me off, but I press my weight down on her, wishing more than anything we didn't have these clothes in the way because I would be inside her right now.

"I'll find out who it was, and I'll make him watch me take your virginity before gouging his eyes out of his fucking head."

Mayson smirks mischievously. "You never asked about that, because who says I'm even still a virgin?"

I lean down. "Me. Because I know for a fucking fact you are, and it'll be proven when my cock has your blood on it."

I rise up off her body, my own protesting the distance I'm putting between us. Even more so as I walk out the door making sure to lock it behind me. I need to force myself to keep walking away. When I get downstairs, I'm bombarded by some girl hanging on me as my teammates give me shit. But all I can think about is the woman I just left upstairs.

CHAPTER 9
MAYSON

When we're on the bus heading back from our away game after our win we're all in good spirits, but then I remember I'm not going home. I'm going back to Colin's house, and after what happened the night of the party the last thing I want to do is face my new roommate.

My previous roommate, and current friend, Blake, sits next to me on the bus. She's also not looking forward to her living situation at the moment either.

"I miss our dorm," I complain.

"Same," Blake grumbles and I know she's not going to go into her complaints with our coach so close by.

I wish we could go back to how things were the last two years. Where Blake and I could peacefully retreat to our room without worrying about shitty stepbrothers, and stupid pranks by the men's soccer team. Where our biggest worries were games and our grades.

By some miracle, I end up falling asleep on the drive back and am jostled awake when Blake shakes my shoulders. I take my time grabbing my bag and walking the short distance off campus to Colin's house.

The sun set about an hour ago, but the street is well lit. I'm used to being aware of my surroundings so I'm not worried about it. Unless a certain six foot two, dark haired soccer player is following me, I know I'm not in any real danger.

The same can't be said for me the minute I step through the front door of my humble abode. Luckily, I don't immediately see Colin so I scurry upstairs to my room annoyed I can't lock it from the inside.

When I unpack and still don't hear him come home I start to relax, but just a fraction. It's enough that I feel I can take a shower without the risk of being interrupted. I'm still cautious, keeping an ear out while I let the warm spray run over me and I wash the feeling of the bus off my skin.

As I'm finishing up, the lights cut out, and I'm completely bathed in darkness. I let out a shriek, and quickly jump out, wrapping a towel around myself as I call out for the man I know is responsible for this.

He doesn't answer and with the power completely out, the silence surrounds me. I pull the towel tighter around my chest, stepping out into my bedroom. It's so dark. So quiet it's eerie. Halloween is still weeks away and yet this is one of the creepier situations I've found myself in.

The irony that I feel more unsafe here in the place I live than I did walking home tonight isn't lost on me.

Opening the door, I peek my head out, calling Colin's name once again into the silent house. I don't want to go down there and risk being even more vulnerable than I already am. As I'm shutting my door, I'm stopped by a hand pushing it open. I immediately try to slam the door on the dark figure currently pushing his way into my room.

"Get out!" I scream.

He doesn't say anything, but he doesn't need to for me to know exactly who he is. He crowds me just like he did the other night. This time I realize the only thing separating our skin is the towel wrapped around me. When I raise my hand to push him away I feel bare skin on his muscled chest. I won't let it distract me as I'm focused on pushing him away, though he doesn't even budge.

Instead of getting him away from me, I find myself falling backwards onto my bed. My only instinct is to tighten my towel around myself because it's the only layer of protection I feel I have. Even though I can't see the man currently straddling my hips as he looms over my body, I can't help but react which only makes me try to buck him off even harder.

"Did I interrupt your shower?" he asks, tracing his finger along the top of my towel.

"No," I insist weakly.

"Good." I feel something cold hit my chest at the same time my towel is ripped open, and I squeal trying to grab for it, but Colin adjusts so his knees are pinning my wrists.

I wriggle trying to get out of his powerful grip, but more coldness falls onto my chest and lower to my stomach.

"What the fuck is that?" I snap, looking and trying to see, but it's useless in the dark.

"Something to get you messy again." He dips down, and I feel his hot tongue lick a line on my chest through whatever he's covered me with. "And delicious."

"What's wrong with you?" I double my efforts to get him off me.

"The only thing that's wrong right now is the fact that I'm not tasting *all* of you," he groans, moving himself lower down my body, holding my hands to the bed while he licks more off my body.

I squirm at the sensation, the hot wet trail of his tongue through the warming...whatever he has on me.

"Get off of me," I protest. Though, I arch up into him as he licks over my nipple.

"I'm helping clean you up again," he taunts, moving lower to my stomach. When he reaches my pubic bone I gasp, and use my legs to try and push him away.

Colin backs away with a hum. "Interesting."

"What?" I snap, hiding my heavy breathing.

"I don't think you've had a mouth down here, have you?" His tone is knowing and I shift around when I think about his questioning the other night.

The questioning he did after he *kissed me.* Not just a kiss either. That was a soul shattering, brutal kiss that I've tried to erase from my memory, and have failed miserably. And no, I haven't had anyone's mouth down there before. Fingers, yes, briefly. But no mouths.

"Doesn't matter, I don't want *your* mouth there," I divert.

He huffs a small laugh, and I know if I could see his face right now I'd want to smack it. "Yeah, you do."

He drops back down to lick my stomach, back up to my chest and over to my other nipple. Before I can register what's happening his mouth is on mine, and his tongue is pushed into my mouth. That's when I taste what he's been licking off me. I want to fight him off again but the taste of whipped cream mixed with Colin has me losing all sense.

He pulls back, and I arch up trying to chase his mouth with my own before I remember who the fuck he is. Then, I drop back, angry with myself, and even more angry that he still has me pinned here underneath him.

"Come to my game tomorrow," he demands.

"Get fucked."

"That's not very nice, *sis.*" He leans down again, his breath grazing my lips as he speaks. "And it wasn't a question. You're coming to my game tomorrow."

"Or what?" I taunt.

"Test me and find out."

I think about my lack of clothes, my lack of independence and the fact that I'm so turned on for my stupid stepbrother that my next words come out knowing the possible consequences, but not even caring. "What else do I have to lose?"

"If you don't show up, I guess you're going to find out."

He rises off me and leaves. I continue to lay on my back unable to move. After several minutes the lights kick back on, and I can see the state I was left in, naked with streaks of whipped cream all over me.

I grab the towel, and storm back into the bathroom annoyed that I have to take another shower. But also annoyed that the temptation to take care of the ache he created between my thighs is so strong. I refuse to do anything to take care of it because I know the only face I'll be able to picture is the man that just left my room.

CHAPTER 10
MAYSON

I hate this.

I mean I love soccer, it's been my life for as long as I can remember and I enjoy both watching and playing it. But being *forced* to attend one of Colin's games is not my idea of fun.

Even if I'll enjoy everything else about it, I don't want to see him. And yes, I could have not come and dealt with whatever retaliation he had planned, but frankly I want my clothes back. I'm getting tired of washing and wearing the same thing, especially for practice.

I debate inviting a friend or two with me, and play it off like we're just watching the guys play for shits and giggles. But the problem is all my friends are also targets for the Rites, so none of them would be safe coming to the game. Chelsey, maybe, because Luca seems to be taking it easy on her.

Or he's waiting and building the suspense. Who really knows with any of these guys because none of them can really be trusted.

Apparently I can't be trusted around Colin because my body is betraying me every chance it gets. I'm a mess and I feel every ounce of it as I pull my ball cap lower on my head while making my way to an open seat to watch the game.

The fall breeze is kicking up, but since I have limited clothes I had to steal a zip up from Colin, which I'm sure he'll be more than thrilled about. The large plain black hoodie only helps me feel like I'm hiding. Even though I'm not doing anything wrong, everything about this feels like I am.

I notice a blonde with glasses wearing an oversized Vipers sweatshirt and looking like she wants to be anywhere else. Which is weird because at Northgate the soccer games are the equivalent to football games for other colleges. Everyone wants to come and be included. But not the girl who I sit next to. She doesn't look up or acknowledge me in anyway, and I wonder if she's here alone. Or maybe she's dating one of the guys on the team since she's clearly wearing one of their hoodies.

Not that I can speak to that since I'm wearing one of Colin's and most definitely *not* dating him.

It's the way she seems uncomfortable that has me speaking up.

"Hi, I'm Mayson," I introduce and she jumps, clearly not expecting anyone to talk to her.

"Hey, I'm Riley."

I nod toward her hoodie. "You know any of the guys?"

She opens her mouth to speak, but then the crowd cheers loudly, cutting off whatever she was about to say, and I look onto the field where the players are running out from the locker rooms. At the same time Riley is joined by a guy carrying snacks.

Of course, the Vipers should be led by their captain, Mads

Keller, but Colin is the first to run out. I roll my eyes at the obnoxious striker pumping his arms in the air as he does everything to draw as much attention to himself.

He scans the crowd during his showboating and his eyes lock on mine sending a chill down my spine. He smiles, clearly pleased I'm here like he asked. I fight every urge in my body to flip him off, but then he winks and breaks our eye contact to focus on prepping for the game.

"Is that your boyfriend?" Riley's question has me cringing.

"God no, he's my stepbrother."

She hums curiously. For a moment I wonder if she's going to ask me more, but she doesn't and I breathe out a sigh of relief.

My focus is purely on the match once it starts anyway. My adrenaline spikes as I watch, just like it would if I was the one on the field playing. I watch their center mid, Reynolds, keeping most of my focus on him since we play the same position. It's always interesting for me to see and compare where I could improve.

The men's game is slightly different than ours, and I recognize that, but I also fully believe my team could be out there up against the guys and win.

The visiting team gets possession, dribbling the ball back toward the Vipers goal. Our winger, Gomez, tries to get possession when they pass, but fails and our goalie, Keller, is locked in waiting for the shot.

They take it, the ball just barely gets past his hand and into the goal. The crowd lets out a collective groan while the opposing team celebrates their win.

For some reason during that moment my eyes find Colin's once again, and see he's already looking up at me, though I don't know why. And not only is he looking at me, but he looks *pissed.*

I narrow my eyes at him, silently asking, *"What?"*

He just shakes his head, raises his chin and then gets back into position for the next play. Again, I hear Riley make some sort of humming noise next to me, but I'm too busy being wrapped up in whatever that just was to care.

It seems like the Vipers losing a goal so early in the game has them more fired up than before, evident in the aggressive playing strategy they adopt. Of course in soccer you can't get *too* crazy, this isn't hockey. But it seems like Colin doesn't care about that because he definitely makes some questionable shoves that the refs don't even call.

The intensity of the game increases and I'm completely locked in. Especially when Colin has possession of the ball, doing what he does best, much to my dismay. He may piss me off but one thing I can't say about him is that he's a shitty player. He shoots the ball toward the net, bypassing the goalie so easily it looks like he wasn't even trying.

This time when the crowd celebrates, Colin hardly acknowledges his teammates. Instead, he turns toward the crowd and looks right to me. I hold my breath in anticipation for whatever he's going to do, but all he does is smile before turning away.

To anyone else it looked like a normal smile. To me, I know that means he has plans. I don't know if I'm more afraid of what those plans could be, or how badly I want to find out.

I hate to admit that it's a good game, and that I actually really like watching the guys. There are a few moments I feel like I would play differently if it were me on the field. I get a sick satisfaction thinking about telling Colin every criticism I have from the game. Even though they won, I have a list I could give him.

I bet he would love that. Biting back a chuckle at the

thought, I see Riley and her friend whose name I never actually caught are standing and waving goodbye.

Pulling my cap down on my head, I make my way out of the stadium and feel like I should go anywhere other than home. I don't want to be around the man I just watched play my favorite sport for the last hour and a half.

Mostly because watching him was more stimulating than I want to admit. I already can't help myself around him and this might make it worse. As I'm walking out, I pull my phone out in search of a different distraction in a group chat with a couple of my teammates.

MAYSON

What's everyone doing?

MAEGHEN

Studying

ANJA

Pretending to study while I stare at this hot daddy at the library *sweating face emoji*

CHELSEY

I'm free.

Well, wait, kinda. I may end up asleep in the next ten minutes because my brain hurts.

None of them are being helpful right now. Blake doesn't even reply and I groan out in frustration. I could go meet Anja at the library, that could be a solid distraction. I'm about to head that way, but my name is called and I know immediately who it is. My whole body freezes; I think about running away, but I know he'll catch me easily.

My body of course is betraying me again because the thought of running and having him catch me makes my legs itch with the desire to do just that. Colin calls my name again, and I turn around slowly, seeing he's still in his uniform with sweat slicked hair and wondering how he got away from his coach's post game.

Then I remember he's Colin and doesn't care about the consequences of anything from anyone.

"Where are you going?" he demands and I fold my arms across my chest.

"Why does it matter?"

"You're supposed to wait for me."

"That was not a part of your super unclear instructions, *your majesty.*"

He smirks. "Nah, I'm not your king, but you can call me sir if you need. Or maybe daddy."

I grimace. "Ew. Neither of those are happening."

"We'll see about that. Go home and wait for me."

"You don't tell me what to do."

"I don't? You came to my game," he challenges.

"Because I want my clothes back."

"And you think you'll get them now?"

I groan, throwing my head back. "Colin, what the fuck?"

"Yeah, babe?" He sounds way too smug.

I shake my head, knowing whatever I'm going to say is not going to help me in anyway. Nothing will ever help me with him and I just need to bide my time.

Though, I'm not one to roll over and just take it either so I can try to play nice but I don't know how long that will realistically last.

"How about you go home and wait for me there. Then we'll see about you getting some of your clothes back."

I bite my tongue to stop myself from spewing all the things I want to say to him, and spit out, "Fine."

I can tell he's riding the high of not just one victory today but now he thinks he just got another. I'll let him believe that for now. Making him comfortable when I push back again will only be more satisfying.

I think I know exactly how I'm going to do it. As I walk back home I think about my plan, it'll be when he least expects it which will make it even better.

Let the games begin, *"brother."*

CHAPTER 11
COLIN

Having Mayson at my game made me play so much harder. Of course that means nothing for the rest of my team, it annoyed the fuck out of me every time the other team scored, or we'd have a bad pass or anyone made a stupid play.

But it didn't matter, not when I looked up to see Mayson in the stands, already looking at me. Even though I know she didn't want to come, she loves the sport. And she likes watching me even though she'll never admit that. Plus, we won in the end.

When I get back to the locker room after chasing her down, Doc is mid speech, and stops to yell at me. "Masters, the fuck did you go?"

"I'm back," I answer instead and I know she isn't happy with my response.

"I see that, but you don't leave before post game. Keep testing me and I'll bench your ass."

I inwardly scoff, knowing she won't but she can threaten me all she wants. Our coaches won't punish us by benching us or cutting from the team because they want to win too badly. But they will punish us in other ways, and I know even our captain isn't immune to it. Especially when it comes to the Rites, so I keep my mouth shut for now, not needing anything to get in the way of the plans I have for Mayson.

I already have her where I want her, and I don't need anything fucking that up.

WHEN I FINALLY GET HOME, the house is dark, and I'm on edge anticipating some sort of trap Mayson has for me. I wouldn't put it past her to do something ridiculous like Saran wrap doorways or the toilet. Maybe next time she'll put bleach in my shampoo.

That's why I showered before I left this time.

Nothing is out of place as I step inside, and I examine my meal prep before heating it up to eat. I laugh to myself, thinking this might have been her plan all along. To make me paranoid and I won't let her get to me like that.

But I can do the same thing. I'm sure she's not sleeping, she's probably in her room anticipating my next move, but there won't be one. At least not tonight. She can enjoy her evening, and I'm sure it'll be anything but peaceful.

I even lay out a couple more articles of clothing for her right outside her door, but still keep her panties. She can enjoy not getting those back while we are under the same roof.

She may think she's winning the battle, but in the end, we both know it's going to be me who wins the war.

The next morning, she's gone when I wake up. I'm angry at first, but then I remember she has a morning class. I think about meeting her outside of it to catch her off guard, but I want to give her a bit of space. I want her to feel comfortable, maybe she'll come to me. She can plan her own cute little revenge if she wants. I'll give her that time.

I want to call her out for not thanking me for giving back more of her clothes, but I know that may be too much to ask for. Which is fine, she'll pay for it later. I'll just add it to my running list.

I head to my own class and sit through the boring lecture, hardly paying attention instead spending most of the class time scrolling through my phone. After the lecture's over, I can't leave quickly enough.

"Colin!" Someone calls my name, and I think about ignoring it, but then I catch sight of a familiar brunette walking in my direction. I don't believe in any of that divine intervention shit, but right now I send up a silent thank you to the universe for presenting me with a solid opportunity.

I turn to the feminine voice that called my name, paste a flirty smile on my face and acknowledge her. "Hey."

"You doing anything later?" she asks in a way that feels familiar like I should know who she is. Maybe we've hooked up before, or she's talked to me at a party, but I have no idea who she is and couldn't even guess her name if I tried.

"Depends," I tease, leaning against a brick wall while making sure Mayson is still approaching. "What're you thinking?"

The girl giggles, looking down at her feet like she's suddenly nervous, but I'm watching Mayson and I see the second she sees me. I lean into this interaction, pretending to be interested.

"I don't know, maybe I could come over again, and," she traces her finger along my exposed forearm, "you know."

So I guess I have hooked up with her before, *great.*

"Hey." Mayson is now next to me, and I give her a lazy look. "You left your sweaty jockstrap in the bathroom this morning, you should really work on cleaning your balls better."

I smirk. "I love how concerned you are with my balls, babe."

Mayson turns to the girl who's clearly sizing Mayson up with a grimace. "You may want to run far, far away from this one."

"And who are you?" the girl asks.

"Don't worry about it. I'm just trying to look out for you, but if you want a plethora of STDs be my guest."

I bark out a laugh, addressing Mayson, practically forgetting we have an audience. "Don't worry about that, babe, I'm always careful."

My stepsister scoffs, shaking her head.

"Yeah, I don't need some jealous ex trying to scare me away, thanks." The girl rolls her eyes and Mayson chuckles.

"You have fun with that, then."

I bite back a laugh as she walks away and the girl is undeterred, but I'm uninterested.

"So, what do you say?" she asks once Mayson has walked away.

"Another time," I lie, standing up and shaking away her touch.

I hear her protest as I walk in the other direction, but that's not my problem. My problem is already walking away from me and I can't wait to see her at home. I just have to get through practice today. Then I don't think I'll allow her to hide from me.

As I'm getting changed for practice, our assistant coach gets our attention, but I'm only half paying attention.

"Don't forget about the fundraiser. This year we're doing a magic show and we want to draw a big crowd."

Some of the other guys start mumbling about it but I just

roll my eyes. The fundraisers are always stupid and this one is more than usual. I'm not doing shit for that, my dad donates enough money to this school that I don't need to participate in some stupid *magic show fundraiser.*

"Hey, how's it going with your *sister*?" my teammate Douglas asks.

"Why do you care?" I snap, already sick of everyone today,. Even more sick of the fact that I'm not back home with Mayson right now.

As my irritation grows so does my need to fuck with her. Or to just fuck her. I know I want to get her desperate for me, I want her to be begging at my feet for me to fuck her, but my patience is running out.

I can only wait so long, especially when I know she wants me, too. I think about earlier today when I was trying to make her jealous. She won't admit it, but I think it worked. And maybe when I get home I'll get the truth from her.

I think about that throughout practice, and it only solidifies my plan even more as I shower and head home.

Of course like everything with Mayson, any plan I have is derailed. Especially when I get home and hear her. I bust through her door, and when I find her with her hand between her thighs, the vibration of the toy mixed with her shriek of surprise, I know I don't stand a chance anymore because if she doesn't get on her knees and crawl to me it's only a matter of time before I do.

CHAPTER 12
MAYSON

I know Colin has class and practice today. Since our practice is over before his even starts the house will be mine alone for a little while. The peace is nice even though I feel like I have a constant electrical surge under my skin. It's just buzzing around while my mind replays the scene of him talking to that girl earlier over and over.

I have no reason to be jealous or feel any type of way about it, and I know that. Yet, I felt *something* and I didn't like it. Of course I was petty, but because he's *the* Colin Masters it didn't matter what I had to say.

But when I think about him, and everything that's happened with him, that feeling under my skin moves down to the spot between my legs and stays there. I want it to go away, the sensation annoys me because I know who the reason for it is and what my mind wants me to do about it.

Looking toward my bed, I chew my bottom lip, but then decide fuck it. I'm alone and horny for no good reason, so I might as well give myself an orgasm to take the edge off.

Maybe it'll help me fight the urge to jump Colin the next time he's close to me.

I grab my vibrator from my nightstand as I lay on my bed. Pushing my pants down, I close my eyes and try to imagine someone other than Colin touching me. I turn the toy on, teasing myself with it while I picture a man—a hot man—running his hands and mouth all over me. I focus on the sensation of the fantasy while the vibration hits my sensitive clit.

As soon as the toy makes contact with my clit I gasp and suddenly, the man has a face, and it's not who I want it to be. I immediately pull it back and groan in frustration. Then, I try again and this time I focus on the feeling more than what he looks like. The lips, both soft and aggressive, moving along my stomach, then lower between my legs. The toy feels so good especially when I imagine it being someone else down there making me feel this way.

I'm so close, but not close enough. The orgasm feels so out of reach, which is annoying considering how turned on I am. That, along with my mind trying to assign my fantasy man a face I give up using my imagination and resort to pulling up some porn. I just need something—anything to help me not think of Colin while I get my much needed release.

Even with the visual stimulation and the toy that's never failed me before, I still just can't get myself there. But I'm so close. The pleasure is just out of reach and I want to get there, which is why I refuse to give up. I focus purely on sensation, what it'd be like if it was me in the video I've got playing while the toy vibrates against my most sensitive nerve.

I let out a small moan, feeling the tingling of an orgasm slowly starting to creep in, it's right there. I feel like I can actually reach it.

Then my door flies open. I let out a small scream, scrambling to hide what I'm doing as Colin stares at me, his eyes dropping down to the spot between my legs and a smile stretches across his face.

"Get out," I command weakly.

He doesn't, because he never listens to me.

Instead, he steps inside, and shuts the door behind him, his eyes not leaving me as he steps closer to my bed.

"Keep going." His deep voice only adds to that fucking buzzing under my skin with those two simple words.

I shake my head, but he steps closer to the bed, and takes my phone from my hand, tossing it to the side. "I'll give you something to look at instead."

I go to retort, but he's pulling his shirt off and my mouth goes dry at the sight of him, shirtless with only that thin chain around his neck. The toned muscles on his stomach remind me how he felt over me, holding me down. The weight of him as he licked the sweet whipped cream off my body.

When his hands drop down to his waistband and he pushes his shorts down I can't help but watch, completely transfixed on the sight in front of me. I haven't moved and I can't bring myself to say anything.

"Keep going, babe. I need something to look at, too."

He reaches into his boxers and lowers them enough to free his cock. As soon as he does, anything else I should say leaves my brain. Seeing his hand wrapped around his large length, pumping it while he stares at me, has the release that has been eluding me suddenly so close I feel like I could explode.

He leans forward, guiding my hand still clamped around the vibrator back between my thighs. I want to smack him away, but then he's standing up straight again, fucking his fist. With the vibration back on my clit I'm about to lose it completely.

"What were you thinking about?" he asks roughly.

"Anything other than you," I manage to say, but it turns into a moan.

"Yeah? Why's that?" he grinds out, tugging at his dick in a way that looks painful.

"Because I can't stand you."

"How about right now? Still can't stand me?"

I shake my head with the lie, all while my hips move trying to chase the sensation the vibrator is giving me.

"You're going to come for me, though, aren't you?" He continues to move his hand over his length, and I hate to admit that it's hotter than the porn I attempted to watch.

The way his ab muscles tense, and veins bulge in his forearms with his movement has my mouth watering. I flood with desire for him, wanting to have his hands on me again, to feel what it would feel like if he was touching me instead of this toy. If it was his mouth on me.

Or even what that huge cock would feel like stretching me in a way I never have been before. It looks like it would hurt, but in the best way. I clench around nothing, my own vagina betraying me with the need to be filled by the man currently jacking himself in front of me.

His eyes are blazing as he watches me and it only heightens every single feeling I'm having in this moment. The elusive orgasm is coming at me full force and all I can think about is Colin and what I want him to do with me.

Normally, when he says anything to me I want to smack him in the face, but I'm so lost in my lust and need that when he speaks, I just want him to keep going. I want him to say more dirty things to me because each word brings me closer and closer to the edge.

"Come for me. Then you're going to tell me where you want me to come. If I can paint those perky tits of yours, or maybe you want me to come on your pussy since it's clearly so desperate for me."

I want to argue, I really do, but I can't. I'm unable to hold back any longer and my head falls back with the strongest orgasm I've ever had.

"Yeah, there she is," I faintly hear Colin groan, but I'm so lost in the pleasure I'm feeling I also may be hearing things.

"Tell me where you want me to come, babe," he grinds out, stepping even closer to me.

I'm struggling to find any words, let alone speak them right now.

"Tell me, or I'm going to choose for you," he threatens, but for the first time it doesn't actually seem like a threat.

Plus I don't know where I would want him to do anything, when I go to open my mouth and say that he cuts me off. "Too late."

He's already coming and the warm sticky liquid coats my stomach and chest. The feeling of it catches me off guard, but what really throws me off is how much I don't entirely hate it. I'm sure it's my own post release euphoria that has me feeling that way, but still I don't move out of the way either.

Even after he's done, I swipe my finger through his release, examining it on my fingers.

"That was fun, let's do it again." He tucks himself back in his shorts while I have yet to move. "You can clean yourself up."

My jaw drops, though I really shouldn't be surprised.

And then he's gone.

CHAPTER 13
COLIN

I'm at the end of my rope with Mayson. I knew I would only be able to handle so much of her around before I would need more. It was the same when we were younger. At that point I was still in denial, and knew I would be leaving for college soon. That I could keep some distance, and not completely lose my mind.

Now it's different.

Now we're adults. There are no parents around and I feel her presence surrounding me *constantly*.

It's only gotten worse the more I've allowed myself to touch her. I see how she looks at me, though her mouth says one thing her eyes say another. I know she's close to breaking. She wants more and I want to give it to her.

But of course we have an away game not long after I got to see Mayson come while she watched me. We haven't seen each other between classes, practice, and now me being away. When I come back everything is going to change.

"Masters," O'Neil calls out while we're on the bus headed to Portland for our game. "What's the plan for Halloween?"

"I don't know. I don't give a fuck about your trick or treating plans," I scoff, not even looking up from my phone. I'm too busy checking to make sure Mayson is where she's supposed to be and not at some random house doing something she shouldn't.

Especially since she *supposedly* has done more with someone that I don't know about. And it's the not knowing that kills me. I don't know what she's done and with who. It couldn't have been in high school because none of the guys there would dare to have touched her. Not after the threats I made sure reached everyone with a dick.

It also couldn't be here at Northgate because I've done the same, while also keeping an eye on her. So who the fuck could it be?

"I'm not talking about trick or treating you dick," O'Neil snaps. I took up at him with the threat clear in my eyes. "You having people over?"

"If I am, then you're not invited," I tell him nonchalantly.

"Yeah, okay," he replies sarcastically. I silently tell him to challenge me on that. I'm irritated enough not being home terrorizing my stepsister and he's about to send me over the edge.

Speaking of terrorizing Mayson, I pull up a text because if I'm not going to be able to do anything in person for the next two days I *will* find another way to drive her crazy.

COLIN
What're you wearing?

MAYSON
Why're you so obsessed with my clothes?

COLIN
Because I can be.

MAYSON

Well, don't worry. I'm only wearing Colin regulated attire since you still haven't given me everything back.

COLIN

And you've hardly done anything to earn it back.

You also better not be adding anymore hair remover to my soaps.

MAYSON

You left everything unattended, it's not my problem if something were to accidently get into it.

COLIN

I've been going easy on you, and it's like you don't want me to.

MAYSON

Do your worst, I can take it.

COLIN

I plan to.

MAYSON

So do I.

I smirk, knowing she will. At this point I'll happily take any silly pranks she wants to play on me. Especially because I have the ultimate one planned on Halloween. She's going to hate it, but it's going to be everything I've ever wanted. And I can't wait.

THERE's one way to get me pissed off beyond belief and that's for us to lose a game. Especially one that should've been an easy win. Portland hasn't won a game all season, and of course the first one they do is against us.

If my team would get me the ball like they're supposed to then I could score like I always do. But of course everyone wants to be the star apparently. Even though that's not their position, and I'm too good to be replaced.

If Mads could stop a fucking ball every once in awhile that would be great.

I wish we would just get back on the road after finishing the game instead of staying the night in a hotel tonight. The last thing I want is to be around any of these idiots. I'd much rather be back home and burying myself inside Mayson. I don't care that she's a virgin, and I don't want to be gentle. I want to show her what she gets from me and give it to her from the start.

She'll take it all, and want more, I'm sure of it.

I pull up her location on my phone again and see she's at home, which fills me full of pride, but she may not be alone. Without thinking about it I FaceTime her, glaring at the screen with each ring that pierces the air around me while I'm alone for now.

Mayson answers with her face scrunched up in annoyance, her dark hair piled on top of her head in one of those messy buns I want to mess up even more. Her bare shoulder is showing from where her shirt is hanging off her frame.

"What do you want?" she snaps, and I notice she's sitting at her desk so I must have interrupted her studying.

"I can't check in on you?"

"Uh no, you can't." She grimaces.

"You answered."

"I thought maybe you were dying, but since you're still alive and well, I'm hanging up."

"You'd care if I was hurt or dead then? Aw, you do love me."

"No," she deadpans.

"You're counting down the minutes until I get back home, don't deny it."

"I'm hanging up now." She ends the call and I bark out a laugh.

I drop my phone down next to me, excited to see what I'm going to come home to tomorrow. If she wasn't already planning something I'm sure she is now.

CHAPTER 14
MAYSON

The house is ready for Colin's return. He's conveniently missing all the laces from his left shoes, so weird how they just got up and walked away. But that's not all.

I've hidden his TV remote and chargers he left behind. I know these are the things that will annoy him the most other than his soccer gear. But of course he took most of it with him, and has left some at school because I couldn't find any.

Then there's the ultimate plan I've set into place. It's the riskiest, but it's also going to have the biggest reward. After what he did with the whipped cream I knew none of my little pranks would be enough. While they're funny and inconvenient just like what he's done to me with my clothes, he's stepped it up and so have I.

I'm gone from the house when he gets back from his away game, and I make sure to stay at the library until nightfall. I'm a little surprised he doesn't reach out to find out where I am like he owns me or has any right to know.

He also didn't say anything about what he came home to,

and the silence is unnerving. Even when I get back to the house, I'm expecting a bigger response from him, but he's just in his room with the music blasting. I scurry to my room, shutting myself in and letting out the breath I didn't realize I was holding.

Colin doesn't try to come into my room or contact me. It only makes me even more anxious not knowing what to expect from him. He's like a predator stalking me in the darkness. I can feel he's there, but there's nothing I can do about it.

Unless I attack first.

I wait until the house is quiet. I'm sure he's tired after the travel and his game which is what makes this even more perfect. As quietly as I can, I take one of his belts I also stole while he was gone and make my way into his room. I don't want to risk waking him up before I'm ready.

I tip toe to his bed, looking down at him in the dark room. He's lying on his back, shirtless with a body that I have no choice but to admire. He's built to perfection, and as much as what I'm about to do is revenge, I'm going to enjoy giving in just this little bit. The little bit that keeps me in control.

Now the hard part. I carefully move his hands up above his head, looping the belt around them and to the bed frame. He stirs slightly and I know if he wakes up I'm fucked. Luckily, I'm able to secure his wrists above his head without him waking up.

Now the fun begins.

I straddle his waist, settling my weight on his hips and swivel, making him groan. His cock starts to harden under me. I bite back the noise of pleasure that wants to come out of my throat at the feeling.

Even though I don't have whipped cream like he did, I lean forward to lick the planes of his chest, tasting the salt from his skin and he groans, mumbling as I trail up to his neck. It's when I sink my teeth into his ear he fully wakes up.

"What the fuck?" He jostles me, and I sit up to steady myself.

"Good morning," I taunt with a smile as he tries to get his hands free.

When he seems to realize what's going on he settles back, and gives me a lazy look. "I wouldn't mind waking up to this more often. I don't know what your plan is, but I like it."

"You won't be saying that for long."

I slide down on his body, hooking my fingers in his waistband and pulling his boxers down to his mid thighs. I can't help but quickly admire the viper tattoo he has wrapping around his thigh. The mouth is open, it should be intimidating, but it only adds to his appeal. However, what is intimidating is his hard dick that bobs free. My mouth still waters at the sight. Even though this won't end how he thinks it's going to, I'll enjoy getting to satisfy some of my curiosity. Especially when I wrap my hand around his length tight enough to make him grunt.

"I don't know what you think you're doing, but in no world will I not like this."

"What if I told you about what it was like when I've done this before," I tease, squeezing around him, moving my fist even as he tenses. "Or I could show you what I learned about using my mouth."

I suck my bottom lip between my teeth, and squeeze even harder making him grunt right before a low growl sounds at the back of his throat. He fights the restraints on his wrists, and I suddenly feel like it might not take very much for him to get free.

"I swear to fucking god, Mayson. You'd better not talk about some other guys cock while mine is in your hand."

"What're you going to do about it?" I move over him again. This time my hips move as well, and the friction from his thigh between them sends a shock through me I wasn't expecting. The feeling has me wanting to do it again, but I don't want to lose my focus too much. This isn't about me and what my traitorous body wants. This is about playing him at his own game.

"I already told you I'd kill anyone else that has touched you."

"Guess you're going to have some blood on your hands then," I say calmly, while I try not to appreciate the feel of him in my hand, and the friction from rubbing myself on his thigh.

He tugs at the restraints once again. I try to distract him by sliding down so my mouth is hovering over his tip.

"I could get out of this, you know?" He raises an eyebrow in my direction.

I stick my tongue out, licking along his slit to taste the salty pre-cum there. "Then why don't you?"

"Because you'll stop, and I'm really curious to see how far you're going to take this."

I hum, and I'm curious how far I'm going to take it too because I was planning on driving him to the edge. But at the single taste and the ache that I've created between my thighs just by rubbing against him has me wanting to push it a little more.

I wrap my lips around the tip of him, keeping my eyes up to watch his reaction. He groans out the hottest, *"fuck,"* I think I've ever heard as he watches me.

While yes, I've technically done this once before, I was interrupted, ironically, by this man right here. He doesn't know it, but he came home and Devon then had to sneak out of the house because I didn't want to clean up any blood.

But this is different in so many ways. For one, Colin is *huge*. He's huge in a way that's concerning for my safety. But I'm not a quitter, and if anything I run on spite and the desire to drive him crazy. Or just plain desire.

With that, I attempt to take more of him into my mouth, fighting the urge to gag when he reaches the back of my throat. I pull back, running my tongue along a bulging vein, up to his tip and flick my tongue over his head.

"What do you think is going to happen when you set me free?" he taunts with a joking lint to his voice.

"Who says I'm going to set you free?" I taunt back right before wrapping my lips around him once again, and suctioning as hard as I can and he groans loudly.

I take pride in the noise I pull from him, and my already damp underwear is soaked with my need to be touched. I ignore it for now, completely focused on bringing him to the edge.

I learn what he likes, what makes him groan and thrust his hips up further into my mouth. Then, when I can tell he's close to exploding, I pull back completely. This time his groan is one of protest. His cock is glistening, wet with my spit, red and angry that I'm not touching him anymore.

He chuckles darkly, and I sit back, taking one more long look at him. He looks like he's sculpted from marble, and no one should have muscles so perfect. No one could have it all in the looks department. Though, I guess what he has there he lacks in personality and human decency.

"Come up here, babe, and let me return the favor," he teases. I hate how instantly tempted I am. But that ruins the point. I'm not going to let him touch me again.

I hum, backing up further. "No, I think I'm going to leave you to finish that."

Colin smirks, looking me up and down. "We've already taken care of ourselves, let's switch it up this time."

"Enjoy...that." I gesture at him while standing up, fighting my shaky legs to remain stoic as I walk away.

"Oh I will." His threat follows me as I walk out of his room, unable to take a deep breath even after shutting the door because I know I've just awoken something in not just him, but myself. Because if I didn't walk out of that room I would've kept going. I would've pushed for more. I would've taken more.

Too bad I don't think leaving the room is going to save me.

CHAPTER 15
MAYSON

I t was wishful thinking that I would have a peaceful night after what I just pulled. Instead, I just ignited a fire that isn't going to fizzle out.

Before I'm able to safely shut myself in my own room, Colin is there shoving his way in. I try to slam the door closed on him, but he's insanely strong, and also angry. Which I know I caused. I'm not as scared of his response as I should be.

He towers over me as he pushes me further into my room, kicking the door closed behind him. I walk backwards trying to get away, or maybe to tempt him even further. I'm not sure which, but with the look in his eyes I feel like I shouldn't push him.

And that only makes me want to do it even more.

"I'm shocked you got out of those restraints so fast." I work to keep my voice steady as lust practically consumes me.

"Told you I would."

"I know, I just mean because you seemed like you were struggling a bit and don't think you've been hitting the gym as much, so—"

He grabs my throat, pulling me into him so hard our chests collide. I try to gasp, but it's hard with the way he's gripping me.

"I was going to let you get away with a lot while living here. I was going to fuck with you in other ways, but you crossed that line babe. Now, I'm just going to fuck you."

"Wha—" I'm cut off when the back of my knees hit the bed. Colin pushes me down. Before I'm even able to register what's going on, he has my pants pulled off my body, and his face buried between my legs. His mouth is latched onto me, working me with his tongue so viciously I screech in surprise, and try to pull away, but he bands his arm around my thighs, and presses his hand onto my stomach, keeping me pinned in place.

He's not taking it easy or teasing me. He's fucking me with his tongue and eating me out like I'm the air he needs to breathe. I'm gasping and struggling because it's all too much, too fast. I've been turned on for so long that having him touch me like this has the orgasm barreling toward me and I feel like I may actually die.

Death by orgasm from my stepbrother's tongue.

Someone make sure to put that on my gravestone.

"Colin, wait," I gasp at the freight train of pleasure headed toward me because I just need him to slow down, it's all too fast and I just feel like I need a second to breathe, or think, or *something.*

"Nope, soak my face," he says it so easily. I'm thrashing around, and fighting that very thing, but when he presses a finger into me while continuing to do actual magic with his tongue, I'm completely gone.

I'm gasping and clawing at the bed trying to hold onto something so I don't completely lose myself as the orgasm pulls me under. I swear I blackout from the pleasure and can feel how smug Colin is about it, which makes me want to smack his stupid face.

Before I'm even fully aware again his lips are on mine in that brutal way he kisses me. His tongue pushing into my mouth, this time the taste of myself on his tongue has the ache between my legs roaring back like I didn't just come within an inch of my life.

I sink my hands into his hair, pulling roughly at the root while I begin to come back to my body once again. I suck on his tongue before biting his bottom lip, meeting the vicious way he kisses with my own. This is a war, but it's one we're fighting with our bodies and it's violent and pleasurable, which has me even more confused.

"You had your chance to stop this, but that time has passed. Now, you're going to feel what it's like to be fucked. Just know that this will be the first and only cock that fills your needy little cunt."

"It'll be the only time so you better make it worth it."

That earns me a laugh. "You won't be able to keep me away once I've felt your perfect pussy squeezing around me."

"We'll see about that." I manage to sound a lot more confident than I am.

Am I really about to lose my virginity to Colin?

Somehow, I know the answer to that and I'm not completely disgusted by the idea.

Not even when he's pushing off his pants once again, his cock that I had in my mouth not long ago is back in my vision. I'm frozen in place, even as Colin pushes my shirt up my body. And I let him.

He pulls the single piece of clothing off me. Then he's laying on me, holding himself up on his elbows next to my head, tangling his fingers in my hair. His hips drop onto mine, his erection is hard between my open thighs.

"I'll go slow at first, only until your pussy is used to me. Then I'm not taking it easy anymore." He thrusts forward, rubbing himself against me. The friction of his cock on my clit has me gasping, and squeezing him between my legs.

He drops his forehead onto mine, moving to rub against me a few more times and I gasp against his mouth that isn't quite on mine, but is close enough it should be. And I can't believe I'm thinking that about *Colin*. That I *want* his mouth on mine. That I *want* him inside me.

I must be possessed by some crazy horny demon if these are the actual thoughts running through my mind. But every time he thrusts against me and I feel that delicious friction between my thighs I get more and more lost.

"You might be my first, but you sure as fuck won't be my last."

Colin smirks, pulling his hips back before pushing forward into me. The stretch burns and I cry out as he sinks more of himself into me, inch by inch.

"I know it hurts, I'll make it feel good in a minute." He pulls back and then pushes in again even more.

I gasp out at the pain once again, but the burn is already subsiding and is being replaced with pleasure.

"That's good, Mace, you're doing so fucking good and you feel even better than I thought you would." He sinks even deeper. "So. Fucking. Tight."

I don't know how he's able to push even further in, but when he pulls out and thrusts forward again I swear he's deeper. My attempts to hold back my cries fail. I can tell how that feeds his ego and it makes me want to kick him.

"That's right, you take me so well," he groans with a strong punch of his hips into mine. Any retort I had dies on my tongue as the moan takes over.

With each thrust, any other thought I could possibly have

leaves my brain because I'm completely consumed in the feelings running through me and *Colin*. I shouldn't want more from him, I shouldn't want any part of him, but right now he's all I can think about. Especially as he pulls every ounce of pleasure my body is capable of from me.

I dig my nails into his shoulders, trying to inflict some pain to him while he's currently about to cause the greatest orgasm I've ever experienced. Even before it's over I hate that it can never happen again.

"I still hate you," I gasp against his ear, as he fucks me harder, rubbing every part of me in a way that has me practically blinded by pleasure.

"You can continue to hate me when I take you from behind next time."

My mouth opens to reply, but all that comes out is a loud moan as my orgasm consumes me completely. My eyes slam shut; I didn't think it was possible to feel so much all at once. All of my senses are completely consumed by Colin. His body on mine, his movement inside me and the fire we've created between us that shouldn't be burning as bright as it is.

He groans, and I feel a foreign sensation as he comes and the small bliss I had from release is replaced with irritation.

"Were you wearing a condom?" I grit out.

Colin smirks. "Why the fuck would I do that? You're going to get used to being pumped full of my cum because that's how you're going to be every day for the rest of your life."

"You're vile," I spit, but it turns into a gasp as he pushes into me even more.

"Yeah, babe, I am. But that doesn't change anything. You're going to continue to be reminded how mine you are, especially when you're so full of my baby in your stomach."

"You're sick. Get off me."

He chuckles, pushing himself up and off of me. The second

he pulls out I feel an odd emptiness right before a the foreign slick feeling is present between my thighs and I realize it's his cum leaking out of me.

I squeeze my thighs together, trying to stop it, right as Colin looks down with a smile. "That's right, keep it all in there for me."

"Ugh," I groan, quickly standing up despite my weak legs and doing my best to ignore the feeling of liquid running down my thighs.

I grab my blanket to wrap around myself while glaring at the all too satisfied man. I start to try and walk away, but realize I probably look ridiculous. Colin's low chuckle practically confirms it. "It's cute watching you try to walk. Like a newborn baby deer."

He stalks toward me, still naked and I see the streak of blood on his cock making my breath hitch. He grabs my throat, pulling me against him again, and uses his thumb to tilt my chin up to look at him. "You marked me too. You're not getting away from me, babe. This is just getting started."

He lets go roughly, and walks toward the door.

"Two can play your sick little game," I call out, but all he does is laugh right before my door slams shut.

I slouch onto my bed, and think about the fact that I did try to play his sick game, and this is how it ended. I was meant to tease and edge him, and yet now here I am, no longer a virgin with my stepbrothers cum inside me.

Clearly, I'm the one that's been played, and it won't happen again.

CHAPTER 16
COLIN

If I didn't leave Mayson's room right away I was about to shut her smart mouth again by throwing her face down on the bed and not holding back this time. I look down at the blood on my cock and part of me doesn't want to wash it off. I want the physical reminder that I'm her first, and her only. I want her to remember it too.

Part of me thought if I had her that this obsession I've had for years would go away and I could get back to normal. But it's the opposite because now that I've felt her hot, tight little cunt squeeze me I want her even more. I want her every second of the day if it was possible.

I want to walk around with her consistently impaled on my dick. I want everyone to know she's full of my cum, and always will be.

The temptation to go back into her room is overwhelming; I know if I don't get further away from her I'm going to burst back in there. I toss on some clothes, and leave the house to go to the campus gym. It's the middle of the night, but I don't care.

I would've thought my body would be ready to crash after finally getting to have Mayson, but I'm more amped up than ever. I blast my music as I drive the short distance, then keep it going in my headphones as I head inside and warm up with a jog. It doesn't take long for me to realize that's not enough and I switch to the weights.

My music is so loud I can't hear the clanking of weights together. Even as my muscles burn and ears are flooded with the heavy music, I can't stop thinking about Mayson's moans, how she looked naked underneath me, head thrown back, her swollen lips open as the breathy sounds left her.

How she was the hottest, tightest thing I've ever felt.

I drop the weight again on my last set, and cover my face with my hands while I try to get my shit together.

One of my earbuds is taken out of my ear, and I stand to punch whoever the fuck decided that was a good idea. My teammate, Walker, immediately hands the headphone back and keeps his hands up, backing away from me like he knows he's two seconds away from getting decked in the jaw.

"The fuck is your problem, Bradford?" I snap, turning the music off so I can hear whatever stupid things he wants to tell me.

"Sorry Masters," he stammers. "Just wanted to see if you're good. I didn't expect anyone else to be here this late."

"I'm fucking fine." I grab my rag from the bench and wipe my face. "Don't ever do that shit again."

"S-sorry."

I storm out of the gym, not wanting to continue to be there if I'm not alone. Which means I'm going back home and I know if I see Mayson, I won't be able to stay away from her.

The house is dark when I get back, there's no sign of her even as I walk up to my room, not looking at her door for too long before I go through my room into my bathroom. As I strip out of my sweaty clothes and step under the scalding spray of the shower I look down to see the water tinge with color as Mayson's blood is washed away.

The sight of it going down the drain pisses me off. So much so that when I get out of the shower, I head straight to the kitchen, unplugging and taking the coffee machine into my room. The best part is that I can lock my door from the inside, unlike hers, so she's going to hate me even more in the morning.

And I can't wait for the fight that will ensue.

THE NEXT MORNING, I wake up from my alarm and glare at my screen seeing the time because Mayson should've left for class already and she didn't come by banging down my door. Unless she overslept; the thought fills me with more pride than it should thinking it's because of me and what we did.

I get out of bed, and check her room. seeing she's not here. I pull out my phone, checking her location and see that she's at class, but she didn't even text me about the coffee machine.

Not taking a chance to lose her shit on me is not like the stepsister I know and enjoy pissing off. Which means I just need to push her a little bit more.

Changing quickly, I jog back downstairs and when I reach for my keys out of instinct I'm met with empty space where they should be in the decorative bowl the designer put next to the front door. I look in and around it, but they aren't there. I open the drawer of the table it sits on to get my spare, and that's gone too.

The laugh that bursts out of me has me shaking my head. The little snake took my keys. Too bad that won't stop me from coming after her. Nothing has and nothing ever will.

I check the garage and see that my car is still there, so she really just took my keys. The thought only makes me laugh harder. I know what she's doing, and campus isn't far away so walking to the building she's in won't take me too long.

Once I get there, I end up leaning against the wall just outside of the lecture hall she's in. It's only a couple minutes before the door opens and people start filing out. Many of them look at me, but don't say anything and I ignore them anyway.

As soon as I see the familiar head of dark brown hair pulled back in a ponytail, I grab her arm, pulling her away from the crowd.

"Wha—" Mayson tries to push me away, but ends up stumbling as I pull her around a corner. "Let go of me, you dick."

I laugh maniacally again, but this time she can hear me. I pull her in front of me, grabbing the back of her neck to hold her in place and force her to look up at me with her narrowed brown eyes. The tiny green flecks in them seem to burn brighter when she's angry like this, and it's only one of my favorite things.

"Would you rather we do this in front of people then?" I raise an eyebrow, knowing full well I'll do it if she decides to push me. I don't give a fuck about confronting her with an audience. In fact, that may be even better anyway.

"Do what? Have you harass me?" she spits out, trying to get me to loosen my grip on her, but it's not going to happen.

"Where'd you put my keys?" I question, knowingly.

She doesn't even try to hide her smirk. "I don't know what you're talking about."

"No? Hm..." I pause, squeezing her neck even tighter. "Maybe I should fuck the information out of you."

"You can *get fucked*, but it's not going to be by me."

I laugh again. "Aw babe, you don't fuck me. We both know how you like to be held down and forced to take it."

"You're disgusting." She tries to get away from me again.

"Give me my keys."

"I don't have them."

"Liar, give them to me."

"I threw them in the dumpster before the garbage came by this morning. Maybe they're still there, go check."

"If you did, I won't be the one searching through the fucking garbage."

"I have to go to practice, so yes you will."

"You think I'm going to let you go to practice?" I smile.

"You don't have a choice. You don't want to deal with the wrath of either of our coaches."

"You underestimate me." I challenge and I can tell how antsy she's getting the longer we stay like this, my hand searing into her skin, holding her in place.

"Whatever. Doc is scary and everyone knows that," she insists and I don't deny Doc can be scary...for other people.

"She's not to me," I insist. "Just hand over my keys, and this doesn't need to be a problem."

Mayson scoffs, reaching into her bag slung over her shoulder, digging around before pulling something out and tossing it down the hallway. "Fetch doggy."

I chuckle darkly, pulling her into me so our chests collide and she huffs out a breath.

"Keep testing me, *sis*, and I'll make you get on your hands and knees following me around the house like my own personal pet."

"Fuck you."

I grip her hip to pull her into me so she can feel how hard I am for her, and she gasps before narrowing her eyes again.

"Yeah, babe. Fuck me."

I let go of her, walking away to swipe my keys off the floor and leave, but that's when I see she only threw one of them, so I'm sure she has something planned with my spare. Which is fine, she can continue to think she's one step ahead of me.

It's all a part of the fun.

CHAPTER 17
MAYSON

"You're distracted," Maeghen notes, and I look down at the ball at my feet that's been there for I don't know how long.

"I'm fine," I insist. Even though yeah, I am distracted.

I have been all day. Hard not to be after Colin took my virginity, then left. Even though I wanted him away from me it stung a little bit to hear him leave the house completely. I don't know where he went, who he saw, or anything, and knowing he just fucked me and may have gone to fuck someone else right after bothers me more than it should.

I know I have no say in what he does. It's not like I even want him ever again, it still made me feel some type of way.

And it wasn't a good thing.

I kick the ball back to her, hardly giving it any effort, and I know she notices.

"Does it have to do with you know who about you know what?" she asks, and I immediately think she's referring to the sex, and rear back because there's no way she would know about it unless Colin has been telling people.

90

Then I quickly realize she's referring to the Rites, not what is done in the privacy of my bedroom. I stop the ball when it comes toward me, dribbling it before kicking it back over to her.

"No, I'm really fine."

I look around to a couple of my other teammates who have been victims to the Rites, like Lucy having her hair dyed green and Blake with her hair blue. I guess that's a positive to having such dark hair, I don't have to worry about that.

Unless Colin decides to bleach my hair or something to make me look like one of the bimbos he usually has all over his dick. The thought has me sick to my stomach because then I'm back to thinking about where he could have gone last night.

I'm glad I brought his keys with me this morning before I left. I thought about driving his car into a ditch or something instead of just taking the keys.

I still could, I do have the spare, but I can't risk myself getting hurt by doing something like that.

"Ladies, line up!" Coach Carmichael calls out and we all line up for whatever drill we're about to run. Instead of being told what we're doing she walks by all of us with our assistant coach trailing behind and I have a feeling we're all about to get in trouble. "We aren't stupid you know."

"What's going on?" Anja whispers to me, and I just shake my head because I have no idea.

"Do you girls think we're stupid?" Coach asks, and I glance around to get any sort of hint as to what this could be about, but my entire team looks just as confused as I do. "I've been at this school for a long time. We all know about the Rites we just choose to let you kids have your fun."

My heartrate kicks up in my chest, worried something big has happened for Coach to be bringing this up to us since it's an unspoken rule and everyone tends to turn their heads.

"You girls have a real shot at winning the championship this year, and I refuse to let some bullshit tradition the *boys team* has stop you all from winning."

No one speaks, but I feel like we're all asking the same silent question. Wondering what he's getting at with this little speech.

"I don't care what you do, or don't do in your free time, just don't let it distract you from what's important. Keep your grades up to comply with school guidelines for athletes and win the games."

We all nod in agreement.

"Good, let's go Vipers," he announces and we move to get into our positions for a scrimmage.

I have no problem focusing on what's important, and what always has been for me. Being Colin's stupid target won't change that. Even if he thinks he has control over me, my time, and my body, he couldn't be more wrong.

I ditch all thoughts of him, because I already started practice distracted enough and I'm not going to let that continue. I'm going back to ignoring him, even if I'm stuck living in the same house as him, I'm not going to give him anymore than that.

Except maybe a few more headaches because we're in the middle of a battle and I don't have to talk to him to fuck with him.

My plan to ignore Colin works longer than I thought it would. I do my best to be out of the house the majority of the day, and when I sneak back in, I go straight to my room.

This goes on for a week, and I feel like each day that passes is a tick off a countdown because Colin will only be so patient.

But every morning I wake up alone and untouched. And every morning my disappointment grows until I metaphorically slap myself in the face because there shouldn't be an ounce of disappointment in my body.

I also still haven't given back his spare key because I'm keeping that as my own insurance policy. Though, the weirdest part of all of this, he hasn't done *anything* to me. No silly pranks, not even talking to me.

Nothing.

Because of that I haven't done anything to him either, though I've been tempted. When he was at one of his games I thought about stealing all of his bedding and make him sleep on a bare mattress with bare pillows.

Then, I considered the fact that he's a man and probably wouldn't even think twice about that.

So I did nothing.

Halloween is fast approaching, and I know any semblance of peace we have is going to end on that day. Everyone knows Colin is going to have a party, and we all know how he feels about me being around for a party.

The good thing about my house actually having a tiny bit of reprieve from him is that I've been able to do what our coach wants, and focus on my grades and soccer.

We won our last game, and are all riding high on it, myself included.

"You coming out with us, Mace?" Blake asks while we're all in the locker room after the game.

I shake my head. "No, I'm tired and going to go ahead and turn in."

"You really want to go home? The last thing I want to do right now is *that*." Blake grimaces and I chuckle knowing exactly why, but luckily for me what was once a torture chamber hasn't been.

The bathtub with a nice soak is calling my name back home. A frat house that's full of sweaty, drunk, and horny guys does not sound like my type of celebration. But my head-phones, some good music, and a relaxing bath, now *that* is how I want to celebrate.

When I get home, it's quiet and I know Colin isn't here, but I've become less and less concerned with where he's spending his time lately because if he's not bothering me then I'm happy. I don't care who he may be with, it's not my problem and if they're keeping him busy then at least he's not seeking me out.

I get my bath started, dumping my lavender Epsom salts in the hot water before stripping off my clothes, and stepping in. I lower myself slowly into the water, letting it soothe my muscles that are already becoming sore from the high pressure game we just played. My music is playing in my headphones while I settle into the water. I drop my head back and my body relaxes.

I'm not sure how long I lay in the water, a handful of songs play and I'm too comfortable to bother moving.

That is, until I sense something is off.

I'm not alone anymore, and my hackles rise. My eyes open, looking to the side I see him leaning against the sink with his arms folded.

Colin is just staring at me, he's in jeans and a dark T-shirt, his dark hair is disheveled in the intentional way he always does. He's looking at me like I'm the most interesting thing in the world, and all I can do is narrow my eyes at him.

"What do you want?"

He says something in response, but I can't hear him over my music. I want to go back to ignoring him, and pretend like he isn't here, but I also don't trust him.

I take out my headphones, and move to cover myself by

hugging my knees to my chest while stabbing him with my eyes.

"Nothing I haven't seen before." He smirks, moving closer to me.

"What do you want?" I repeat.

"Already told you."

"I couldn't hear you."

"That's not my problem."

I glare harder. "Get out."

Instead of doing what I want him to, because he's Colin, he steps right up to the side of the bathtub and kneels down on the floor. He rests his arms on the edge, while his eyes stay locked on mine. I expect them to roam over my body, but he doesn't break the intense eye contact and it makes me squirm under his gaze. His dark blue eyes seem even darker right now, and I do everything I can to hide my shiver.

Clearly, I don't do a good job because with the way his eyes darken even more I know he can sense what he's doing to me. He knows exactly what to do, and unfortunately for me I'm the one that's most vulnerable right now.

"You've been avoiding me," he states.

"So have you."

"I'm not now."

"I wish you would."

Colin dips his fingers into the water, swirling them around, slowly dipping them lower into the water until he's grazing my thigh, and moving up and down my skin. I watch, unable to move even though I know I should. My body reacts against my will at his light touch. It's primed, remembering what it's like when he really wants to touch me.

The way I want him to right now.

"Do you? Because you're not leaving," he taunts.

I swallow roughly, wanting to get out and away from him,

but also wanting his hand to move up higher. To move to the sensitive spot between my thighs that's already aching for more from him, even though I was sore for days after he fucked me. I crave it again, even though I shouldn't.

"You're in my way," I tell him weakly.

He looks from side to side. "There's plenty of room for you to leave. I'm not stopping you."

His caresses on my thigh don't let up, and even as he says he's not stopping me, I feel like I can't walk away. I don't look away from his hand because if I do then I'm going to look at his face, and that may be worse. Especially right now as his hand is getting dangerously close to my pussy.

"If you want to leave, Mace, leave." His voice is gravely, and only adds to my internal conflict.

I shake my head.

"You're not going to leave? You're going to let me touch you again?"

I swallow again, looking up through my lashes and nod once.

"I know you want me to, babe, but you're going to have to do better than that to make it happen."

My jaw drops as he stands up and leaves without a second thought. All I can do is drop down into the water and refuse to come back up for the foreseeable future.

CHAPTER 18
MAYSON

When I finally emerge from the bathtub, my fingers are wrinkled and the water is cold. I manage to get dressed and climb into bed. Another night passes where Colin doesn't make another appearance, and I wonder if him coming into the bathroom was really just a dream.

The next morning, when I get downstairs, I'm greeted by him in the kitchen. The sight has me stopping in my tracks. He's cooking wearing only sweatpants and a cut off shirt that shows the bottom part of his back. When he turns around to face me the glimpse of his abs is mouthwatering. So much so I'm questioning my entire existence.

He shouldn't be allowed to look this good. His muscled frame in just pieces of fabric, but looking so obscene makes me want to scream.

"Good morning," he greets with a smirk, like he knows exactly what he's doing.

"Where's the rest of your shirt?" I ask, trying to divert and hide how hot I find it.

He just shrugs, shaking his protein shake. The way his muscles bulge with the action has me rolling my eyes, if only to look away for a second and try to regain my composure.

I continue to avoid eye contact with him as I go up to the coffee machine he finally put back for me. Even as the drink brews, I refuse to look at him. Which is getting more and more difficult as I feel his eyes on me. I do my best to act unaffected by him, his proximity, and the tension that's constantly surrounding us.

When I feel his heat at my back, I stand up straighter. Then his weight is pressing me against the counter and I bite back a small gasp. I try to keep my hand steady as I pour the coffee into my mug, and I'm impressed with myself that I manage not to spill anything.

Until he presses completely against me, the counter digging into my hips while I feel how hard he is against my ass. His lips are against my ear and I freeze. "Do you wish I touched you last night?"

"No," I lie.

"You sure about that?" His hand grips my hip, and starts to move along my waistband, dipping inside just barely.

"Yes," I squeak.

"What about right now? Do you want me to touch you?" He asks. His hand moves lower, cupping me and I feel the rumble from his groan as his mouth grazes my neck. I hardly even notice the way I'm leaning into him.

"N-no," I stutter, even as I press myself into him even more.

"No?"

"Mhm," I hum because my body is reacting in one way, but my mouth keeps saying what I should be saying.

He runs his mouth along the side of my throat, and I lean back against him even more. My hips buck against his hand as he presses the tip of a finger against my entrance and I moan, gripping the edge of the counter tightly.

"Do you want more? I know you do, but I want to hear you beg for it."

My mouth opens, but no sound comes out and he pushes his finger into me just barely and I gasp, holding onto the counter even more because I feel like if I don't I'm going to collapse.

"Beg," he growls against my ear, thrusting the tip of his finger in and out, but it's not enough. I want more, but can't get any words to come out.

I rub myself against him even more, still unable to speak.

"If you don't want it, that's fine." His teeth nip my earlobe and I lean into him even more. Then he's removing his hand from me and I let out a silent protest, catching myself on the counter.

I turn around to glare at him, doing my best to steady my breathing and not show how affected I am. Just as I do, he puts his middle finger up, and wraps his lips around the tip I know was just inside me.

"Can't wait to taste more of you again." He takes his protein shake and walks away. "Have a shitty day, sis."

I continue to stand in the middle of the kitchen, catching my breath, too wet for my own good and it's all because of him. I should follow him just to punch him in the face, but I know that's not what I would end up doing and I need to leave this house as soon as possible.

Abandoning my coffee, I debate leaving the house in my pajamas, but I know it'll be too cold so I quickly run to my room to change and race out of the house.

Once I'm outside I feel like I can breathe for the first time. The house is stifling with the sexual energy in the air and I need reprieve. My class doesn't start for another hour, so I go to the café by campus to get myself a coffee since mine was rudely interrupted.

When I'm waiting for my drink my phone goes off, and when I see who texted me, I glare at my screen.

COLIN

Just say the word and you can have my cock again, babe.

I grimace, locking and putting my phone back in my pocket. I may turn into an idiot around him, but I'm going to stay strong, and things won't go as far as they have ever again. Maybe if I keep telling myself that, I'll believe it.

BEFORE PRACTICE, we're all in the locker room getting changed and it seems like everyone is in a mood. I don't know if it has to do with the Rites, our upcoming game, or just general school stress.

Blake is next to me, and nudges my shoulder. "How's it going with you? I feel like we've hardly talked."

"I know, I don't like it." I shake my head. Since we lived together the last two years, not spending so much time together is weird for us.

"Are you liking your new roommate?" she goads.

I give her a look that I hope portrays, *"what do you think?"*

She chuckles and I shake my head.

"You know what he did this morning?" I ask. "I found him in the kitchen in a fucking crop top and sweatpants. How slutty is that?"

"I love a man in a crop top."

Same.

"Give me a crop top and a slutty thigh tattoo on a man and

it's over," our teammate Lucy adds. Unfortunately, my step-brother has both.

It's like a lightbulb goes off in my head and I smile over at Blake. "I have an idea."

After quickly sharing my plan with my team before practice—and without our coach finding out—we have a very limited amount of time to get it done. Luckily, the guy's locker room isn't far from ours and no one should be in it for at least another 30 minutes after we're done with practice.

We all skip out on our shower and rush over there as inconspicuously as possible. In theory, it doesn't sound that hard, but sneaking fifteen girls into the men's locker room is actually a bit more difficult than it sounds. Some of the girls on our team opted out of participating, and I think they aren't targeted by anyone for the Rites. *Lucky bitches.*

Blake peeks in and signals that it's clear for us to storm in. We only found a couple pairs of scissors, so we move quickly to cut into their shirts, and rip them the rest of the way. We work quickly, tossing the shirts into lockers they never lock when we're done.

After we're all done we leave as quickly as possible. I head back to our own locker room with a few of my teammates to shower because I want to stick around to watch how this is about to turn out.

"Are you going to watch?" I ask Blake.

"Of course I am." She smirks and I can see that she's about to get the same pleasure of watching as I am.

"Me too!" Chelsey shouts excitedly.

"Yeah, I'm here for them playing practically shirtless," Anja adds.

"I wouldn't miss this for anything," Maeghen joins.

I already know this is going to be fun.

The girls think they're so fucking funny.

After Reyes pulled out his shirt and looked at it like he should know why it's suddenly missing half the fabric, we all start finding the presents the girls left for us. Most of the guys just shrug it off, not caring that we're going to be practicing with half shirts on.

I don't give a fuck, but knowing this is because of the girls makes me want to laugh and go punish my little captive. But I know there's a reason for this, and if they want a show then I guess that's what we're going to give them.

"Anyone know who the mastermind behind this was?" Mads asks.

"I have a guess," I grunt.

We all head out to the field, and just like I expected a handful of the girls are in the stands watching. Including Mayson. Her elbows rest on her knees and she holds her chin in her hands with a self-satisfied smirk on her face. I turn in a circle to give her a full view before shooting a wink at her.

"Alright, we're—" Doc stops what she's about to say when

she looks at all of us in exasperation. "I don't want to know what caused this, why or have any part of it. Run your drills and don't be idiots."

There're murmurs from all the guys as we look up at the girls. I don't know what everyone else is thinking, but I'm mentally making plans for mine.

"Your girlfriend going to have a problem with the girls team ogling you?" Vito ribs Reyes.

"Nah, she knows what she has," Eli replies confidently and I roll my eyes. I don't know what happened that he suddenly didn't want to be a part of the Rites and had this new girlfriend *after* it started. It seems weird as fuck to me, but whatever.

Mads is glaring up at the stands, and I don't know who he's looking at, but as long as it's not my girl then I really don't give a fuck.

After some of the guys are being idiots trying to put on a show for the girls, we all get serious for practice. I can tell how irritated Doc is, knowing something is going on and that it could affect our game. But nothing is enough to distract me, not even Mayson. I'm too good at what I do, it's like second nature to have a ball at my feet. And when I'm done, it's second nature to have Mayson underneath me.

Which will happen again soon, I know it. She wanted me last night and this morning. I don't even need to push her for it, she *wants* me. I knew leaving her alone for a little while would only make her want me more. And that's exactly what I wanted.

After practice is over, I look up and see the girls have all left already, and I'm sure Mayson is going to try to avoid me again, but it's not going to work. She better be home by the time I get there because if not I'll go find her and drag her back.

Luckily, when I get home the lights are on so either she's home or she wanted to make it seem like she is.

When I walk in, I hear her music playing and I wonder if I'm about to find her in the bathtub again. As much as I would love to take advantage of having her naked in front of me, part of me hopes she doesn't make it that easy for me.

I did make one stop on my way home at the Halloween supply store because as annoyed as I am about the expectations of the upcoming holiday, I have plans for my roommate. I toss the mask I bought on the counter before making my way upstairs to find her.

I'm thankful of my past self that changed the lock on her door to only lock from the outside before I brought her here. I knew I wouldn't want her to be able to restrict my access to her. As much as she wants to deny it she wants me to have that access.

When I try to push open the door, there's resistance like she put something in front of it. I push again, and it's clearly something large, my guess is her dresser. I chuckle at her attempt to keep me out.

"Mayson," I call out between the crack in the door.

"I'm busy," she calls back over the music, and my blood boils.

"Open the fucking door," I demand.

"No, my guest won't like that very much."

Guest? What the fuck?

"I don't give a fuck. Open the door."

"Nope, like I said, I'm busy."

I strain my ears, listening for any other voice, but the music is so loud, if they're speaking quietly I won't hear them. The only thing I can think of is that she's in there with another man.

And that's enough to set my blood on fucking fire.

I ram my shoulder into the door, feeling the object give

slightly. I know it'll only take a couple more before I can bust in there.

"It'll only be worse if I have to break down the fucking door," I threaten, ramming into it again.

"I swear to you, Mayson, if you have a guy in there he's dead and then I'll take care of you in a different way."

Another ram into the door.

One more, and I'm sure I'll have enough room to get in.

I give her a few more seconds to make a decision, but I'm done being patient. I've been forced to have her around me for years, unable to do anything about it and now here we are and I can do whatever I want.

One more solid push and the door is open enough for me to get into the room. I look around, searching for anyone else that shouldn't be in here, but it's just Mayson. She's sitting on her bed, she looks a mixture of mad and smug. I take in her appearance because I know what my girl looks like freshly fucked, and she's clearly not. Her hair is wet from the shower, and her clothes are in place while she sits with her arms resting on her knees, glaring at me.

"Where's your *guest?*" I sneer, searching the room for any sign of another person.

She just shrugs. She. Fucking. Shrugs.

"Mayson," I say darkly, slowly starting to stalk toward her. "You said you had a guest, so where is he?"

The side of her mouth quirks. "I never said it was a guy."

"Then where is *she?*"

Again, she shrugs.

And that's what does me in. I'm on the bed, pinning her down within a second as she tries to fight me off.

"You can't keep manhandling me. Get off," she squeals as I continue to pin her wrists to the bed, with my knees framing her hips.

Mayson is trying to wiggle and kick underneath me, but it doesn't work, and she knows it won't. We've been in this position before, and yet she still thinks it'll be different.

"You like it when I manhandle you, and if you were in danger then whoever your *guest* is can come and save you."

"I'll scream."

"Please do."

"Why're you so disgusting?"

"Why do you like it?"

She snaps her mouth shut, going right back to glaring at me, but I know there's no real heat behind it. The only thing she's telling me with her eyes is how badly she wants me.

"Tell me something." I lean over her, bringing our faces close together, our chests touching so I feel the rapid rise and fall of hers. "Was this *guest* going to touch you?"

"Yeah, they were going to do everything you'll never get to do again," she spits.

"That so? They were going to slide their hand in your pants, and feel how wet your needy little cunt is like I did this morning?"

"Yup, but it would be even more wet for them because they *aren't you.*"

I chuckle. "Yeah? Some faceless, nameless person can make you come better than I can?"

"*Anyone* can make me come better than you."

"You're such a bad liar," I huff, maneuvering myself between her thighs and pressing myself against her even more. "You think I don't know how you enjoyed watching me practice in a half shirt?"

"I don't know what you're talking about."

"Oh babe, we really need to work on your lying." I shake my head, sitting up. Before she can even register what's happening I flip her onto her stomach and press my weight against her back.

She flails around clawing at the bed and trying to buck me off, but it's not going to happen. And we both know it. I press my hand between her shoulder blades as I get to my knees, making sure she doesn't go anywhere.

"Don't move," I tell her. "I'm going to prove to you and whoever your mysterious guest is that the only person who can make you come is *me*."

CHAPTER 20
MAYSON

I think I'm going to admit myself into some sort of brain research facility. Because the way that I continue to get stupid around Colin should be studied. I feel like I blacked out and have ended up underneath him...once again.

I knew nothing would stop him from getting in here, but I wanted to at least try. That's why I pushed my dresser in front of the door since I can't lock the stupid thing from the inside. I also knew he would be on a rampage after practice since he would know we were behind the prank, and goading him about having a *guest* was the icing on the cake.

What I didn't expect was to be in a position like this once again. Face down on my bed with Colin commanding me not to move. His hand on my back has prevented me from doing so, but he's moving lower, and I don't even want to move.

His fingers hook in my waistband, pulling my shorts down, and of course I'm still without underwear because he hasn't given me any back. I've been finding random pieces of my clothes throughout the house, but still no fucking panties, and I know he doesn't intend to give any of them back.

The cool air hits the skin on my bare ass as he pulls my shorts off, and then his warm hands are sliding up my thighs and onto my cheeks, kneading them roughly.

I wiggle, not sure if I'm wanting to get away, or trying to entice him to touch me even more.

"Fuck, babe, I don't know why you think you can keep yourself away when you're dripping for me."

I can't help myself from saying something I know will set him off. "It's not for you, it's from your whole team. Watching you guys like that fu—" I'm cut off when his mouth latches onto me, roughly licking completely from my clit to my ass.

I squeal and lurch forward as soon as I feel his tongue there. It's surprising, and should feel wrong, but I'm fighting the urge to push back against his mouth even harder because it feels anything but wrong.

"You really just like to push me, don't you?" he asks against my pussy. "I'm going to prove to you once again the only person that can make you come is your fucking stepbrother."

I scoff, wanting to be disgusted with him, the situation, and the position we're in. But his mouth is on me again, licking me completely and everything that isn't a moan fades into the background.

He pulls back, his hands gripping my ass tightly, pulling the cheeks of my ass apart then I feel a foreign warm wetness fall onto my skin, and I gasp.

"Did you just fucking spit on me?" I gasp.

"Yeah, baby deer, better get used to it." He groans and then his mouth is on me again, and this time he doesn't let up. I don't even get a chance to complain about the nickname. His tongue is everywhere, roughly eating me out from behind. I should try to get away, but it feels too good to move anywhere that isn't closer to him.

I bury my face in the bed, muffling my moans as he fucks

me with his tongue. The vibration from his groans against me heightens my arousal to impossible levels. I want to fight against the pleasure so badly. I want to prove to him that he isn't as great as he thinks he is.

But unfortunately for me, he *is* as good as he thinks he is and I hate that even more about him. He's as good looking as he thinks he is, he's as good at soccer as he thinks he is. And he's as good at giving me pleasure as he thinks he is. But that's probably the worst one.

Especially when his teeth sink into my thigh and I cry out at the pain. He's pushing a finger into me and curling it to rub my inner walls and I'm so close to losing it as the orgasm is threatening to consume me.

"Tell me again, who else could make you feel like this?" he goads.

I shake my head, not wanting to say anything. I just push myself harder against him instead, trying to chase the pleasure and not think about who it is that's giving it to me. I don't have to see him, so I can pretend it's not Colin that's touching me and giving me these feelings. Except he keeps talking, making it impossible. Even if I try to picture anyone else, it's his face, his body, his hands on me, his mouth. It's always him.

"Admit it, Mayson."

I moan louder into the bed as he works to pull every ounce of pleasure my body is capable of.

"Admit that you want me and I'll let you come."

I avoid saying anything, just trying to force the orgasm myself, struggling to breathe against the blankets but I don't care, it only heightens my pleasure.

"Admit it or I stop," he threatens, fucking me harder. His thumb presses against my asshole and I suck in a sharp breath. "Admit it."

I'm so close, I'm right there, I know I can get there before he pulls away. I know I can I just need another—

He starts to pull away, and I gasp in protest, grabbing his arm. "Please, I want you, please."

He chuckles softly while he thrusts two fingers into me. I cry at the sudden stretch. "Damn right you fucking do. Now come for me, show me how fucking pretty you are when you scream."

And I do. Without hesitation, without holding back, I let go and let the pleasure consume me as I combust, knowing full well who it is I'm letting do this to me. Knowing full well there's no going back because I just told him I want him. It can only get worse from here.

I'm catching my breath as I come down from the powerful release as he lazily pumps his fingers until I'm squirming again. "Colin," I complain, trying to wiggle away from him, but not because I actually want to, but because I'm overstimulated.

"Fuck yeah, keep saying my name," he groans right before removing his hand and then slapping it down on my ass. The sharp feeling is surprising and I cry out, quickly rolling over to glare at him.

He's leaning over me almost immediately, his mouth less than an inch from mine and I'm completely frozen having him look at me with such intensity, his lips so close to touching mine I can practically taste it. The fact that I want to taste it is only adding to the insanity I've fallen victim to.

"You want me," he states smugly. It's not a question. We both know what I said. Even if I already want to take it back.

"You wanted me first," I retort, feeling childish for the response but my brain isn't able to come up with anything better right now.

He leans even closer, our lips brushing as he talks. "Yeah, I did. And I still hate you for it."

Then his mouth is on mine, and I'm unable to process what he just said because he's kissing me. His lips on mine, his tongue rubbing against mine as he kisses me like a punishment. My teeth sink into his bottom lip, and he groans, pressing himself into me. His hard cock rubs against me and suddenly I want him again. I hate that I respond so easily to him. He's still Colin. He's still my stepbrother.

He guides my hand down to his length, his hand covers mine as he silently instructs me to squeeze him all while kissing me like I'm the air he needs to breathe. I move my hand along him and he groans into my mouth. I do it again because I like the thought of driving him insane too, but then he's parting our mouths and I try to chase it.

"You'll get my cock again, baby deer, but now it's your turn to know what it's been like for me."

"What the fuck does that mean?" I sit up, watching him get off my bed and back away toward my door.

"I waited to have you for years, and now knowing you want me it's your turn to wait."

My jaw drops. "That makes no sense. Now because I want you, you don't want me?"

Colin chuckles. "Keep saying it, I fucking love how you sound admitting it."

"You're giving me whiplash."

"Good. Get ready for Halloween, I want you in something with easy access." He winks and I grimace.

"This is your only chance to have me. If you leave this ends," I threaten weakly.

He laughs. Full on laughs because he obviously knows I'm bluffing, but I don't understand this game he's playing. Is it only fun for him if he's chasing me? Fuck. That.

"No, babe, this is just getting started."

CHAPTER 21

COLIN

I deserve some sort of award for not fucking Mayson every single day since the first time. It's amazing I've managed to survive and stayed away as much as I have. But then she told me she wants me. I *still* managed not to bury my cock so deep inside her she would feel me for weeks. Even though I want to see her stumble around like a baby deer again.

I want to make sure the next time I fuck her, it's going to prove just how mine she is. Not just to her, but to everyone. I want to make a statement loud and clear that Mayson Dunne is *mine*.

Everyone has been on my ass about Halloween, I finally said I'd have a get together at my place, but I'm not supplying shit. Which doesn't matter to anyone because kegs appear, people bring their own drinks and whatever the fuck they want to all my parties. I'm not hosting shit like my mom used to. This is a college party, I don't care if you don't have a good time.

Speaking of my mom, she's hardly even checked on me since I moved in with my dad when I was sixteen. My dad, on the other hand, just sent me a text, though it's not even about me.

DAD

How's your sister? Her mom is worried.

COLIN

Stepsister. She's fine.

Your son is fine too, thanks for asking.

DAD

I know you're fine, I don't even need to ask.
Mayson is a good girl, her mom worries.

I scoff, if only they knew what a *good girl* little precious Mayson is.

COLIN

She's living with me now, she's safe.

DAD

Good. You better be nice to her.

COLIN

I'm always very nice to her.

I let her come and didn't even force her to take my cock down her throat for all her fucking sass. I'd say that's pretty nice of me.

DAD

You both are coming home for Thanksgiving.

COLIN

I know.

He doesn't say anything else. There's nothing left to say, and I toss my phone on my desk. I don't need it tonight, I know where Mayson's going to be, and she's not leaving my sight. Hell, she's not going to get away from me once I catch her later.

The only plan I have has to do with a mask, her, and the forest that surrounds our house.

She's at her friends right now, but I know they'll be back soon, and I'm going to be ready. I'm already on edge when I hear some of my teammates bursting through my front door, already being obnoxious shits, especially Reyes. The loud fucker.

Music starts blasting and more people start to show up. Even though everyone is in costumes, I recognize most of my teammates. A majority of the girls didn't even try with their costumes, just the cliché lingerie and some sort of animal ears or lace masks.

I have my skull mask on. It hides everything except my eyes as I stand back against the far wall facing the front door, just waiting for Mayson. I'm in a black hoodie and dark jeans, arms folded across my chest as I glare in the same direction looking for that one particular woman.

My woman.

I noticed Reyes and Mads are both in masks as well. Those two were the only ones I had to double take to figure out who they were. Of course as soon as I heard Mads' accent I knew right away it was him.

My attention falls to the door currently opening and the group that walks in. Front and center is none other than the one I've been waiting on. Her dark brown hair falls over her shoulders in waves as she wears a dress that's so tight it looks like it's molded to her, and splattered in fake blood. I have no idea what or who she's trying to be, but I don't give a fuck. I plan to have it shredded by the end of the night anyway.

She's got some of her teammates with her, and I stay back, just watching and waiting for the right moment. She gets drinks, laughs, but I make sure she doesn't talk to any of the guys around here. She doesn't seek me out, which I'm both happy about and pissed off because she should want to know where I am.

I let her have her fun for a little while, but not too much. She can never have too much fun unless it's with me.

When she goes to get her third drink, I decide it's time to step in. I may have drugged her that first night, but I didn't touch her. I want her aware and an extremely active participant when I fuck her again. I crowd against her back at the kitchen counter, pressing my hips into her perky ass as I lean down to speak into her ear so she can hear me over the noise.

"Don't even think about it," I threaten.

Mayson turns her head to the side so I can see her profile, the fake smeared blood on her jaw and onto her neck makes me want to lick it off. "You don't tell me what to do."

"We both know that's a fucking lie." I thrust my hips forward to push her even harder against the counter. I swear I hear the smallest little mewl come from her lips. "Here's what you're going to do, if you want to be my good fucking girl tonight. You're going to go outside without drawing attention to yourself."

"Oh, that's not going to work for me." She sighs, turning around even though I don't move away from her at all so her chest is now completely against mine. "See, you said if I *want* to be a good girl, and I don't. Especially not for *you.*"

I chuckle. "That's not what you said the other day."

"A moment of insanity."

"Nah, that was the truth baby deer. You're going to be my prey. Now you can make this easy, or you can continue to pretend to fight me."

She glares at me, and I see that she's conflicted, but I also know she's going to give in.

"Either go outside, or I have no problem chasing you out there right now."

She clenches her jaw, slams her cup down on the counter, and glances over at something behind me. "Let me grab a knife first."

"I'd let you cut me up if that's what it takes." I wink.

"You're fucking awful."

"You can keep insulting me, I like that too."

"Ugh," she groans, pushing at my chest, and I let her move me back a step just to see what will happen.

Either she's going to listen, or she's going to make me chase her out of here. I don't mind either option. I'm going to have my fun, and despite what she might think, she's going to have some too.

She storms over to the front door, not doing a great job of not drawing attention to herself, but I don't care. She goes outside, and I follow. My eyes stay glued to her ass in that skin tight white dress with the red splatters all over it, and I want to get her even dirtier. I want to see her skin covered in the fake blood, dirt plus my cum and spit. I want her fucking filthy.

The thought has me stomping forward, following her out into the cool night air. There's a few people out front smoking, but I don't pay any attention to them because my eyes are focused on my stepsister who's walking toward the dark trees.

My eyes catch on another one of my masked teammates following someone out in a similar direction as me, and I see I'm not the only one with this idea, but I can't blame him either. Who doesn't like a little primal play?

Halloween is the best time for it. Masks, mystery, and the allure of being whoever you want to be. Even though with her I want to be Colin and Mayson, and I want her to feel the same. Which is why I want her screaming my name loud enough the entire party can hear her from out here.

She glances back over her shoulder. I see the moment she notices how I'm stalking close behind and her pace picks up.

She stumbles slightly on the wedge heels she has on her feet, and I'm waiting for her to ditch them in the dirt.

Especially when I pick up speed, and she notices. We're getting past the tree line, the light from the surrounding streets is getting dimmer the more we move into the forest. I'm glad the mask doesn't obstruct my vision. But I wouldn't let anything stop me or slow me down.

"Better start running," I threaten darkly, and for once, she listens. Kicking her shoes off, she takes off. I love how fast she is. I know she runs to keep up her endurance for soccer and that makes the challenge even more enjoyable.

It'll make the moment I catch her even sweeter.

CHAPTER 22
MAYSON

Realistically, I know it's Colin that's currently chasing me with that hot as shit skull mask on his face. But my brain can't seem to register that I'm not in any real danger. Though, knowing that it's Colin may be even more dangerous than if it was some deranged psycho. Because the deranged psycho is actually my stepbrother.

I may be able to outrun him, though. I'm pretty fast, and I'm smaller than him. I could probably find some stump to hide in or something if I get far enough ahead. I'm not wearing the best outfit for this, I thought the white dress with fake blood all over me would be something different. I thought I was creative being a murder victim, but I feel like it'll make me an easier target than I already am by the man chasing me.

I kick off my shoes because they're only going to slow me down, and I take off. I do my best to ignore the dirt and sticks stabbing into my feet as I run, focusing purely on getting away. The cold air whips at my face as I quickly make decisions on where to turn and weave.

His thunderous footfalls are behind me, and I can feel how

close he is, which is way closer than I want him to be. I try to pick up the speed, but my lack of shoes is hurting me more than I expected it to. I do my best to black out the pain of my feet and continue to run.

Despite my effort, I can feel him gaining on me and I know he has the advantage of living here longer and of course the actual shoes on his feet. I turn quickly, hoping it throws him off, but all it does is make me lose my balance and then I'm flying face first into the dirt with a scream.

I try to scramble to my feet and get away, but his weight is on my back, pushing me down. I try to fight to get him off me, but it's useless with how he maneuvers my body with ease like he's done every single time we've been together.

"That was cute, baby deer, I really thought you might actually make me work for this tight little body this time." He doesn't even sound out of breath and I want to knee him in the balls for it.

"There's still time," I say weakly. At the same time he's pushing up my dress revealing my bare ass.

Yes, I could have bought more underwear today when I bought this dress. Yes, I could have bought more almost any time since this has started, but for some reason I haven't. And I'm not about to delve into the psychology of why I haven't.

"I can't wait until the day I fuck this too." Colin groans, slapping his palm onto my skin sharply.

The thought has my fight returning as I try to buck him off because I've seen his dick. I've felt it once and I know how massive it is. And I know that thing is not fitting in my ass without me ending up splitting completely in half.

"Don't worry, Mace, that's not happening tonight. But I am taking this pretty little pussy again." While that should have me fighting, it doesn't because I've been desperate to feel him again ever since that first time.

I expected him to give in and fuck me a lot sooner than right now, but instead he's chosen to tease the shit out of me. Now here we are, and I have no fight in me when it comes to him fucking me again.

"Oh you want that, don't you?" he taunts.

I swivel my ass around, desperately wanting some sort of friction even though I'm currently face down in the dirt while my stepbrother pins me down, and is currently pushing his pants down. I hear the rustling behind me, and I don't think I've ever wanted this more.

His hands find my hips and pull me to my knees so fast I have to catch myself with my palms in the dirt and leaves on the forest floor. I dig my fingers in, trying to hold onto something as I feel him teasing the head of his cock along my seam.

"You're so wet for me. Do you like being chased or is it the mask?"

"Neither," I breathe, trying to push back against him.

"So this is just because of me then?"

No, it's because you and the mask and I never realized being chased was so sexual. And also I may be completely fucked in the head.

He grabs my biceps, pulling my arms behind me, holding my forearms folded on top of each other in one of his large hands, and uses it as leverage to pull me onto his dick with one hard thrust.

I cry out at the stretch, wanting so badly to hold onto something, but he's holding my arms hostage as my knees already ache from the ground.

Colin groans loudly as he stays fully seated inside me and I gasp for breath as I adjust to his size. I swear he feels bigger this time.

"You feel even better than I remember," he moans, pulling back an inch before pushing back in completely once again.

I want to agree, but that would admit too much to him.

He uses his hold on my arms to pull me back against him over and over, slowly at first then starts to speed up as my moans get louder. I feel used in the absolute best way, like I'm just a toy for his pleasure as he fucks me into him, my ass slapping against his thighs with each powerful thrust.

"You don't think you're a good girl, but you look like one right now. *Fuck,* you should see how good your cunt looks stretched around my cock like this."

I hate that I want to see it. I hate that I want to see his masked face while he fucks me into oblivion. I hate that I feel the orgasm so close I can practically taste it. I hate that despite everything, I want him and he knows it.

"You're going to come for me like this, and then we're going back home and I'm going to fuck you for the rest of the night. I want you so full of my cum it's dripping out of you during your game tomorrow," he says like a threat.

"Colin," I moan, not sure if I'm complaining, or wanting more.

"I know." His fingers dig into my skin so hard I'll probably end up with bruises on my arms.

My knees are going to be bruised for sure, and I hardly notice the tears streaming down my face as my release gets closer and closer. I'm gasping, moving back against him, unable to fight any of this. It's pointless anyway.

"You've got this," he encourages, and for some reason the subtle praise and encouragement is what tips me over.

I'm crying out. The only thing holding me up is Colin's grip on my arms as he continues to fuck me, harder and faster until he finds his own release. I feel him swell inside me followed by the feeling of being filled once again.

"So fucking good," he groans, the sound muffled by his mask.

He lifts me up as he stands, and I don't even fight his hold as he carries me back toward the house. I can't even think about how I must look, and what people will think when they see us like this. But at the same time I really don't care.

He fucked all the fucks out of me, I guess.

I'm sure my teammates are going to have questions, and they'll be ones I don't have answers to, but I don't care.

Part of my brain also worries about someone taking a picture of whatever state I'm in and posting it, but then I remember who the man carrying me is. And he would never let that shit get out. He might be crazy and evil in a lot of ways, but he would kill anyone that tried that.

For some reason, that thought has me nuzzling my face against his chest, burying my nose in his hoodie. He always smells so good, but right now that woodsy cologne is mixed with the real woods and sex and it leaves me wanting him once again.

I hardly notice when we're back inside with how quickly we go up to his room. The sounds from the party are muffled as soon as the door closes behind us, and I don't know what I expect to happen from here, but I can't deny that whatever it is, I want it to. We've moved past denial and while I'll never stop fighting him, I can also enjoy how he makes me feel. Which is too damn good.

CHAPTER 23

COLIN

I tuck Mayson against me as I walk us back to the house. The party is still going, but if anyone tries to say anything to me, I'll punch them square in the mouth. All I care about right now is getting my girl up to my room and taking care of her over and over for the entire night.

And maybe into the morning.

And all day.

In fact, maybe I won't leave her body for the rest of our lives.

My mask is still on, even though I want to rip it off so I can take her mouth with mine. I want to bury my face in her sweet little pussy before pumping her full of my cum once again. I want to take her in every position known to man so I can make her come from every angle and see how many different ways I can get her to fall apart for me.

No one pays us much attention as I walk through the people in our living room and up the stairs. I kick and lock the door behind me. Everyone can get the fuck out at some point.

They know better than to try and stay here longer than they should.

Mayson lifts her head, realizing where we are and seeming to become somewhat aware instead of her blissed out post orgasmic state she's been in. She starts to wiggle out of my hold, and I let her so she can come face to face with my mask.

The top of her head barely reaches my shoulder as she looks up to me, covered in fake blood and dirt. The stick in her hair and mud smeared on her perfect skin makes the blood look even more real.

"What're you even supposed to be?" I finally ask.

She looks down at herself, like she needs to see it to remember, then looks back up and shrugs. "A murder victim."

"Why?"

"What're you?" she diverts.

I tilt my head to the side. "What do you want me to be?"

Her eyes narrow, clearly not happy with my answer, but it's true. I didn't have anything specific in mind, I just wanted a mask and dark clothes to chase her down in. Other than that, I'm whatever she wants me to be.

"My first instinct is to say, 'gone.'"

"That's not going to happen, try again."

"Figured," she scoffs before her eyes trail down my body, and then her hands are on my stomach, pushing my hoodie up. I raise my arms so she can push it all the way off. And I let her.

Her fingers trail along the indents of my abs, tracing them and I let her explore because her hands on me feel so amazing. I want her to go lower, touch me everywhere, and she does. Unbuckling my belt, and unbuttoning my pants, I go to remove the mask, but she stops me.

"Keep it on," she commands and I want to argue with her, but then she's guiding me to my bed, and forcing me to sit down. The thought of her having some control over me turns me on more than I thought it would. Just like the other week when she tied me up and blew me.

If she wants me to keep the mask on then I'll do it for her.

I sit, leaning back on my hands, waiting for what's going to happen next.

Mayson reaches behind her, unzipping her dress and letting it fall onto the floor. I notice some of the small scratches and bruises starting to form, marring her perfect skin. I know she's going to wear them like a badge of honor and I'm filled with pride knowing I'm the reason they're there in the first place.

She reaches behind her, unhooking her bra and adding it to the pile on the floor while she stands completely bare in front of me. My hands clench with the desire to grab her hips and yank her on top of me, but I try to be patient.

It pays off because Mayson steps closer, placing her knee next to my hip, then the other one, straddling my lap. When her weight settles on me I wish more than anything she'd taken my pants off before having me sit here. And then she swivels her hips, and I grab her skin to hold her still.

"You can't be naked and on top of me without riding my cock right now," I tell her, seriously.

"Aw, are you desperate to feel my pussy again?" she taunts, and I tighten my grip on her hips.

"Careful," I threaten. "I'm letting you have some fun, but you know I could throw you onto this bed and do whatever I want with you. Again."

She shivers, and leans forward, pressing her forehead against my mask as she rubs herself over me once more.

"Take the mask off," I growl, wanting to feel her mouth on mine. I want to taste her skin, suck her nipple into my mouth, impale her on my cock and watch her ride.

"No, I'm going to fuck you, but I want the mask to stay on."

126

My hand moves to her throat, collaring it there and the move causes her to rub herself against me even more. I know she loves when I hold her like this.

"You can fuck me now, but the rest of the night I get to have you however I want."

"Chasing me in the forest wasn't enough?"

"Doesn't seem like it was enough for you either." I tighten my hand on her throat, just enough that she can feel it.

"Maybe you're not as great as you think you are."

"We both know that's a fucking lie. Take my cock out, babe, I want to see you ride it."

She swallows against my palm, and reaches down. Her hand spears into my pants, gripping my cock that's rock hard even directly after fucking her the first time tonight. She squeezes, pulling me out of the confines of my pants, and I lift to push them down a little more to have extra room.

Mayson positions herself over me, swiping my dick through her wetness, looking down between us to watch the action. She moans when the head hits her clit and I want to push her down completely on me, but hold myself back, just barely.

Her palm lands on my chest, pushing me down on my back and I go, keeping my eyes on the spot where we're almost connected as she continues to tease my cock. I hold her thigh, needing to touch her while my other hand snakes up her body to pluck at her tightened nipples that I want to suck into my mouth.

Her hips buck, bringing the tip of my dick even closer to feeling her tight wet heat once again.

"Come on, Mace, put us both out of our misery and drop your wet little cunt onto me."

"Beg for it." She smirks.

I grip her thigh tightly, and the sensation of her warmth on my tip, knowing just how amazing it feels to be buried inside her, is enough for me to let her have this. Just once.

"Please," I grit on. "Please, let me bury myself in this perfect pussy."

Her jaw drops at the same time as her ass and I'm back in the softest, tightest, wettest pussy I've ever felt. I groan, moving both my hands to her hips and digging my fingers into her skin as she stays still, fully seated on me adjusting to the stretch.

"Tell me how it feels," I groan, wanting her to say something to distract from my need to come way too soon.

"So good, so fucking full, you're so *deep*." She moans and maybe it was a bad idea to have her talk because hearing her say that has me closer to release than I was before.

"Damn fucking right I am, and you better get to riding so I can feel you come on me again."

Her hand slides up my chest, up to my neck where my silver chain is resting against my skin. She hooks her finger in it, twisting it once around her finger and moving it to the side so the metal bites the skin of my neck. I lift my chin, showing her I want more. She could fully choke me right now and I'd take it. I'll take it all as long as she stays just like this, on top of me while I'm buried inside her.

"I like this," Mayson comments, moving her finger along the chain.

"And I like this," I slap my palm down on her ass.

She yelps, bucking her hips forward, rubbing herself against me. I grip her ass tightly, trying to guide her movements over me. I want her to get herself there just like this while I hold back from filling her up once again. And when I do fill her up, I'm going to push my cum back in so she stays full of it.

"You like this too." She lifts up, then drops back down

while bracing both her hands on my chest, pressing her weight down on me.

"Fuck yeah I do." I flex my hips up to fuck up into her even harder. She digs her nails into my chest and I groan at the sensation. She's everywhere, the weight of her, the smell of her, my life has been completely consumed by Mayson since the day she walked into it. And it'll continue to be that way for the rest of our lives.

She lifts up again, then back down and works up to a steady rhythm she gets lost in. I join her, letting her do what feels good because everything she's doing feels fucking amazing to me. I keep groaning out praises while she rides me. I can't help but fuck up into her, slamming our hips together when I feel her getting close.

"There you go, babe," I moan, bringing my thumb to her clit, rubbing it exactly how she needs.

When she squeezes around me so tightly, I know she's close and it's a good thing because with the way she's strangling my dick there's no way I could hold back much longer.

"I'm—" Mayson moans.

"I know you are, do it."

She does, letting go, coming with a cry as she continues to buck on top. I grab her hips, moving her the way I need while I thrust up into her and then I'm joining her release with a loud groan of my own.

Mayson collapses onto me, her head dropped to my chest, breathing heavily while our bodies are still connected. I don't want to move from this spot, and she doesn't do anything to move either. So we don't.

That is, until Mayson reaches up to push the mask off my face, and then her lips are on mine, and just like that, I'm lost in her once again.

CHAPTER 24
MAYSON

Halloween shifted things. I don't want to admit it out loud, but in my mind, I know it has. The next morning when I wake up still wrapped around Colin, I don't immediately want to get up and run away. I stay as long as I can, but then reality kicks in. I have a game this afternoon, and a mountain of homework.

I slip out of Colin's bed, and he groans, turning onto his stomach. His arm stretching out on the mattress where I just was, but he doesn't wake up. With a sigh of relief, I sneak into my room and my phone is already lighting up on my nightstand where it's plugged in, which is something I didn't do.

The thought that Colin did this brings a weird warmth I shouldn't be feeling to my chest. I pick it up and see several texts from my teammates, and when I scroll through my eye catches on one from my mom.

MOM
How're you doing?

MAYSON

Fine.

MOM

Is Colin taking care of you?

More than you'll ever know.

MAYSON

I'm an adult, I don't need his help.

MOM

He's your older brother, it's okay to have his help.

MAYSON

STEPbrother. No actual relation.

MOM

Family is family, Mayson.

No, it's not, mother.

MAYSON

Agree to disagree.

MOM

You both are coming home for Thanksgiving. Walter said he spoke to Colin about it already.

I scoff because I know it's expected, but of course no one has said anything to me about it.

MAYSON

Okay.

MOM

And I have someone I want you to meet.

I grimace at the screen, not even wanting to entertain whatever it is she's planning. I move over to another text thread with my concerned friends that apparently saw me being carried in by Colin last night.

BLAKE

If you don't respond by ten A.M. I'm calling the police.

MAYSON

No police needed, I'm alive.

ANJA

My money was on death by dick.

MAEGHEN

I guessed you were being held hostage.

CHELSEY

I said you were having a great time. *shrug emoji*

MAYSON

All of you are wrong (mostly) but I'm fine. Focus on the game.

ANJA

Are you going to be able to walk, let alone play later?

MAYSON

middle finger emoji

I toss my phone onto my bed, then look down at myself, seeing the fake blood, dirt, and probably some real blood all over me. Not to mention the stickiness between my thighs that gives me an extremely vivid reminder of everything that was done last night.

I beeline to the shower, needing to feel clean, and do my best to erase the touch of Colin from my skin. Not because of shame or disgust. But because I can't afford to be distracted later, and I don't know what any of this means with us. I don't know if this means the pranks will stop. I don't know if this means we're together, or if spending the night together in one of our beds is going to be a regular occurrence.

I don't know any of it. That's why I can't focus on that right now because we have a game to play. And win.

WE'RE GETTING into position for the game, I'm moving my legs to keep them warm as I wait for kick-off. Blake and the other team's forward are in the center circle, neither is saying anything in anticipation for the game to start. I'm a little surprised Blake is even here after what happened on Halloween. But her dedication to soccer is unmatched.

Once the ball is in play, everyone jumps into action. Blake wins possession of it, and we go into attack mode. As a center midfielder, I both attack and defend, so I jump into assisting with the attack as we run into the opponents side of the field. Blake kicks the ball over to me, I dribble it, but pass it to Chelsey when a defender is on me too much to have a clear shot.

One of our passes is intercepted and the other team gets the ball, driving it to our side of the field. I have to switch gears into defending.

I've always liked how fast paced soccer is. I get to lose myself in the game and my sole focus is on scoring and making sure the other team doesn't get a chance to.

The ref blows their whistle to pause the play when one of the other players goes down. It didn't even look like they were hit very hard, but they stay down, and we use the time to catch our breaths.

She ends up getting taken off the field, and we reposition after they get one of their alternates on the field to fill in her spot.

We get the first goal after a few more minutes of play, and we celebrate with Blake who was the one to score it. It's always a morale booster to get the first goal of the game, and I feel revitalized going into the next play.

Anything else that doesn't pertain to what is happening on this field right now doesn't matter. Even though at one point I look up in the stands and I swear my eyes catch on a familiar pair of blue ones. I look away before I can distract myself even more. But for some reason the thought of Colin being here watching the game has me playing even harder than I normally would.

Not because I want to impress him. Because while he may think he's the best at everything he does and that he's a god amongst us all, I want him to see that I'm also the best at what I do. He just happens to brag about it and I'm more humble about it.

One of us has to have some humility.

We end up winning the game, and when I take the time to look up in the stands again, I can't find the dark blue eyes I swear I saw earlier, but I don't care. I'm sure he'll be home when I get there. I'm sure he won't leave me alone for the rest of the night.

And with the high I'm riding from the win, I don't want him to.

Maybe he can pull out that mask again. I would have never imagined that would be as hot as it was. I never thought about being chased in the forest, especially my by stepbrother in a mask.

Yet, it was the hottest thing I've ever experienced and I wouldn't mind if he wanted to do it again. And again.

Which makes me think of all the other things I've heard about, but never thought I would be interested in. With Colin, I'm open to so much more than I ever would have thought. I've imagined what it would be like to wake up to him touching me. What would happen if he came home while I was in the kitchen, didn't say a word, tossed me on the counter then ate *me* instead of whatever I was cooking.

The fantasies are out of control. And I don't think there's any chance of them slowing down or stopping any time soon.

CHAPTER 25

COLIN

Ever since Halloween, I've made sure to have Mayson in my bed every night. Even when she tries to fight me on it, we both know she doesn't mean it and she just ends up there anyway. I've even watched a couple of her games, but I don't think she knows that.

I also gave back her clothes. Still no panties, and I added some lingerie she has yet to put on for me, but she will. Especially if I don't give her a choice.

We're about to head to our parents' house for Thanksgiving. I thought about taking everything out from the bag she packed and only put the lingerie in there.

But I'll be fucking damned if my dad saw her like that. He's an asshole, and while I don't think he would ever touch her, I don't want to even put the temptation there.

Mayson and I have been in bed together every night, but she's still my target for the Rites. I like fucking with her, and don't plan on stopping. Which is why the pranks haven't stopped, on either of our ends.

The other day, I overheard someone talk about hermit crabs in a bed. I thought about it, but since I've forced her into mine, I didn't want to put them there. Sadly, that prank will need to wait for another time then. Or someone else will need to do it.

My main focus is annoying her by taking things she needs so she comes to me, complaining and angry. Then I put her in her place, fuck her the way we both need, and she can get whatever it is back.

Her pranks continue to be a little more brutal. I've hidden the scissors and I'm not giving those back since cutting my clothes is her go to and has been even when we were younger. Though, I know now how much she likes watching me walk around in a half shirt.

I did catch her putting bleach in my shampoo, which ended with her being bent over the side of the bed, my handprint left on her ass right before I fucked her mercilessly.

It's a great life.

Heading back home to where I first saw Mayson has me feeling some type of way. Knowing we're going to be under the same roof as our parents and that I won't have the freedom to touch her like I do now already has me on edge. I could probably make her come to my bed with me anyway.

Who gives a fuck if they find out what we're doing. We're adults. We aren't really related. And my dad has never actually given a fuck to what I do anyway. Her mom may be another story.

But I also don't give a fuck what she thinks either. The only reason she's with my dad is because his money, and anyone with eyes can see it. The only good thing she's done is bring Mayson into my life. Though that could be considered a bad thing since I've never been so obsessed with someone until her.

In a way she ruined my life by walking into it because I'll never be the same, especially now that she's really mine.

We had early morning practice, and the girls have theirs after us. I'm home now, loading up my car so we can drive back home after she gets back. She doesn't know that's the plan, but Thanksgiving is tomorrow and I don't want to deal with driving in the morning.

I grab her bag, rifling through the contents to make sure she didn't get new panties and sneak them in there. I'm surprised she hasn't but I have a feeling my girl likes going without them so she can hop on my dick whenever she wants. Tossing the bag into my car, I remember the lingerie I've left out, and vow to make her wear them when we get back. Especially the little maid one, and maybe I'll make her clean the whole house in it.

Now that's an idea.

I see her approaching as I close the trunk, and she tilts her head to the side. She's so fucking gorgeous, it's ridiculous. She's always been pretty and anyone would have to be blind not to see it. Her long dark hair, especially pulled back in a ponytail like this swinging behind her. The light brown eyes that always have a fire in them when she looks at me. Toned body from the rigorous soccer schedule. Strong legs that can squeeze the fuck out of me when I'm buried deep inside her.

Yeah, my girl is fucking perfect.

"What're you doing?" she questions.

"Loading up, and you have perfect timing, we're heading out."

"I thought we weren't leaving until the morning?"

"Never said that. We're leaving now. That a problem?"

She chews on her lip like she's weighing if she wants to say something, but then shakes her head. "Nope. Did you grab my bag?"

"Yes I did."

"Did you take all my clothes out of it?" She narrows her eyes at me.

Thought about it.

"I didn't touch it."

"I don't think I believe you."

I shrug. "You want to check?"

"Kinda."

I open the trunk, gesturing toward it. "Go ahead."

Her eyes narrow even more. "I feel like this is a trap."

"How would it be a trap? You were questioning me. I *nicely* packed up the car for us to go to our parents' house for the holiday." I fold my arms across my chest, and lean against the car.

"Ew." She grimaces. "Don't say *our* parents it makes this sound so incestual."

"What is *this?*" I question with a raised eyebrow.

"You know." She points to me, then herself, then back and forth. "This."

"Us? Like us together?"

"Mhm."

"Like the fact that you're impaled on my cock every single night, screaming my name while I make you come harder than you ever have before?"

She slams the trunk closed, grumbling, "Go away."

I bark out a laugh at her mini outburst because I love how she still gets weird about the thought of us together. I don't know if it's because she's still trying to convince herself she hates me, or because we're step siblings. Or because she only likes my dirty talk in the bedroom. And she fucking *loves* it in the bedroom.

We get in the car, and she immediately takes over the

music selection, which I'm fully prepared to argue about, but the first song starts to play, and it's one I actually like.

"What?" she asks, already defensive.

I shake my head. "Nothing. But if you start playing Taylor Swift, we're changing it."

Mayson tries to hide her smile, but I catch it before she looks away, mumbling, "You know you like Taylor Swift."

I drive us away from campus, and neither of us say anything initially, just the sound of the music that sounds like it could have been taken from one of my own playlists. Part of me wonders if she really did take some of these songs from me, but I doubt she would admit it if she did.

"What do you think of road head?" I ask once we're off campus, and headed toward Mercer Island.

"Uh, sounds dangerous."

"You don't trust me?"

She laughs loudly. "No. I do not trust you. In no world do I trust you."

"That's too bad because I trust you." I glance over at her.

"Yeah, okay. We're literally in a prank battle because of *your* teams tradition. You shouldn't trust me."

"Well I do, because what's the worst thing you're going to do to me?"

"I could think of a few things," she grumbles, sinking lower in the seat.

"Yeah? I told you to do your worst, babe, and yet I don't think you have."

She huffs, and I can tell I'm getting to her, so I push harder because that's what I do.

"You could really get me back by coming over here, and taking my cock in your hot mouth."

"I'll pass," she grumbles.

"You'd rather wait until we get home? That's fine too, baby

deer. I may want to finish in your pussy rather than your throat anyway."

"We are not having sex this weekend." She's trying to be stern, and it's cute.

"You are so quick to jump on me every day, and you really think I'm not touching you all weekend?" I can't hide the humor in my voice at the thought.

"I am not," she rears back.

"Right," I reply sarcastically. "And neither of us are going four days without you tackling me."

"I would never *tackle* you. Get over yourself."

"You better behave. Can't have mom and dad catching us," I taunt.

"Don't be gross." She slaps my shoulder, and I laugh even harder.

The rest of the drive is fairly lighthearted and easy. Even though she continues to insist we won't be fucking this weekend, she's about to learn how wrong she is. I may be joking about her jumping on me, but really we both know neither of us can stay away.

CHAPTER 26
MAYSON

When we get to the giant mansion, I shake my head just like I do every time I see this place. It's crazy how we went from living in a tiny apartment to this. It's never felt like home, but really nowhere has for me. We moved around too much and while this was the most stable place we lived, it wasn't *ours*. It was never mine. It was us moving into someone else's home and inserting ourselves into their lives.

Which Colin made sure to make extremely clear when we met. And ever since. I don't belong in his world, in his house. Or with him.

Except lately, it's felt the opposite and I don't know what to do with that. He's always made it seem like he hates me and wants nothing to do with me. I fully realize whatever we're doing is probably temporary and that he's just using me for sex. That he wanted that level of control over me. Maybe it's all some extra level to the Rites that the guys are doing.

I don't know, but it's why I'm not letting myself get too

invested in this. No feelings. I could never have feelings for him.

The sex is nice. More than nice. It's better than I could ever imagine, and that only makes me want to guard myself even more.

Especially right now as we walk into the house. Colin's carrying both our bags, and I wasn't going to argue because he can be my pack mule. I'm independent, but if he wants to carry my shit, then he can go right ahead.

"Mayson!" my mom exclaims when we walk into the large open house and she sees us. She sounds way more excited than she usually is when I've come back from school. Immediately, I know there are guests here.

I'm proven right when we walk further into the entertainment area and see a woman around my moms age and a guy that has to be around mine.

"Welcome home, sweetie." She pulls me into a hug I'm slow to return because we've never been overly affectionate and I hate when she puts on a show like this in front of other people.

"Uh, hi," I hesitate.

"Be nice," she whispers so only I can hear, then speaks up. "Come here, I want you to meet someone."

She guides me over, and I look over my shoulder to Colin because I don't want him to leave me alone with this mess. He drops the bags before trailing behind us. I can already see the anger burning in his eyes, and I worry this may take a turn very quickly.

"Mayson, this is my friend Nancy and her son Garrett." She beams while introducing them.

"Hi." I wave awkwardly. Nancy looks me up and down and I can see her nose wrinkle. Though, it looks like more of her face would do the same if it could move under the face lifts and botox.

I know I'm not dressed well, fully aware I'm in sweatpants and a baggy T-shirt with my hair thrown up in a messy bun. But it's not my fault, I didn't expect strangers to be here on our first night back for a holiday.

"Nice to meet you." Garrett steps up to me, taking my hand and shaking it. I can feel Colin's death stare without even looking back at him.

For some reason it has me pasting on a wide, fake as shit smile when I respond, sweetly. "Nice to meet you too."

"Your mom has been telling us all about you. She said you were pretty, but you are drop dead gorgeous." He grins, and I feel Colin step closer to my back as I smile at Garrett.

"I'm Colin, what has she said about me?" His deep timbre takes over the space. He covers my back with his chest, reaching around me to extend his own hand toward the new guy.

I fight the urge to sink back against Colin. Instead, straightening my spine, but I can feel his other hand grip my hip. I bite back my reaction because I'm not sure if everyone can see how he's holding me, but it's not very subtle.

"Oh, uh, n-nice to meet you too. Haven't heard much about you," Garrett stutters and I want to laugh at how nervous he is. If only he knew Colin is not someone to be afraid of, even if he thinks he is.

"Hm, interesting." I can see how tightly he's squeezing Garrett's hand before he lets go.

"Well no offense, Colin, but he isn't here for you," my mom says with her tone trying to be lighthearted, but it only has me tensing. She clearly doesn't know what she's saying or who she's talking to.

His hand tightens on my hip even more, and I don't know if

anyone other than me has noticed that he hasn't stepped away from my body. "Then why is he here?"

"Be nice," my mom scolds. "Nancy is my friend, and I thought Garrett and Mayson could get to know each other. Is that okay with *you?*"

I don't even have to look back at Colin to know his face is completely still, blue eyes flared with anger. "No. It's not."

My mom just laughs lightly like it's a joke, but I know better. "Oh, stop. Anyway you two go take your stuff upstairs and then you can join us."

Colin pulls me into him, and guides me out of the room, grabbing our bags and continues to walk behind me as we walk upstairs. As soon as we step into my room he shuts the door, drops the bag, spins me around, and pushes me up against the door, caging me in with his hands on either side of my head.

"What the fuck was that?" he sneers, and I bite back a smile because I'm clearly deranged.

"My mom being my mom." I shrug, and he clearly is not happy with that answer because he presses closer to me, closing off any escape I could have possibly had.

"You going to entertain him?"

"Maybe, it's not like anyone can stop me," I goad.

"No? You don't think I'm against bending you over the table down there, and making them watch as you scream my name with my cock buried deep in your needy pussy."

"You threaten that, but I know you wouldn't let anyone see me like that. Maybe you should do that and prove it."

"You don't believe me?"

"Not even a little bit."

"Hm," he hums, pressing his hips against me, and I can feel how hard he is already. "Maybe I want to see how far you'd be willing to entertain that idiot because we both know you wouldn't let him touch you."

"I wouldn't? I'm not a virgin anymore. Maybe I want to see what else is out there."

I'm poking a bear and fully aware of it, but so is he. We're just poking at each other and we both are too stubborn to let up first. I don't have any interest in Garrett. He's okay, but with his pushed back hair, button up, and lanky frame, he looks too put together for me. I like them with messed up dark hair, covered in sweat from playing soccer, tattoos on his thighs and a chain around his neck.

I want him dangerous, and forbidden. And standing right in front of me testing my limits.

"Sure, okay. You go down there and entertain them, and when you get bored you'll be on your knees begging for my cock again."

I scoff. "You really are so full of yourself, you know?"

"Yeah, but you love being full of me." He rubs himself against me just barely. "Go have fun, but you'll be screaming my name by the end of the night."

"We'll see about that."

GARRETT. Is. Boring.

Holy fuck, I didn't know it was possible to be this bored.

The worst part is I know Colin's loving every second of this because he can read me better than anyone and no matter how hard I try to hide my boredom, I'm sure he can see it written all over my face.

Apparently Garrett is a couple years older than me and already working at his dad's business doing...businessy things?

I don't know, I really zoned out as soon as the word "spread-sheets" was said.

"Isn't that great, Mayson?" my mom said, way more excit-edly than someone should be about this conversation.

"*So* great." I fake smile at Garrett. It's probably not his fault he's so boring, he just is.

"I had an idea, would you two like to go out to dinner sometime and get to know each other a little bit more?" my mom asks like it's the greatest idea she's ever had.

Garrett looks at me. "If you'd like to, I'd love to take you out."

"Yeah, Mayson." Colin's booming voice feels louder even though he's speaking normally. "Would you like that?"

I glare at my stepbrother, remembering our challenge earlier, and knowing it's only going to piss him off more when I say, "I'd love that."

I expect Colin to glare at me, or dive across the table we're sitting at to beat Garrett's face in. But instead, he smiles. It's that one that looks sinister. And promises that I'll be the one paying for it later.

But I'm not scared, even though I probably should be. It's too much fun to mess with him, and I always end up winning in the end anyways.

CHAPTER 27
COLIN

My dad comes home while I'm sitting through my own personal hell. Listening to this fuckwad talk about himself and shit that no one cares about, especially Mayson and me. She pretends to be interested, but I can see the way her eyes glaze over. Then she agreed to go out with him, and it's funny she thinks I'll actually let her go.

Maybe I will, but I'll make sure to send her out with her cunt full of my cum. She still doesn't have any panties so it can drip down her legs while she sits there pretending to be interested in whatever boring shit he's talking about. That may be more torture for her than me making sure she doesn't go.

Now that's an idea.

But all thoughts about that are derailed when the man, the bane of my existence, Walter Masters walks in.

"I didn't realize we were having a party," he announces, attempting to joke. Mayson's mom, Juliette, laughs but the two of us just stare at them.

"Walter, nice to see you again," Nancy greets, and Garrett

stands up to shake my dad's hand. The kid likes doing that apparently. I thought about crushing the bones in it when he shook mine, but I held onto Mayson instead and used her to ground me.

"What all have I missed?" my dad asks the group. He looks around, not making eye contact with me, which isn't completely surprising.

"Garrett and Mayson are going to go out. Isn't that exciting?" Juliette beams. Now I know I make a face, but the only person that catches it is my stepsister.

"How great, you two would make a great pair," he says like it's some partnership and not a relationship.

I scoff, unable to help myself. "What would you know about that?"

"Excuse me, son?"

"What would you know about a 'great pair'? You a relationship expert all of a sudden?"

"I'm very happily married to the perfect woman, so I'd say yeah, I am."

"Really? You sure you don't need to find...*extracurricular?*" I see him tense, but tries to hold it together because there's company.

"You don't know what you're talking about, and I advise that you stop now, son," he threatens through gritted teeth.

I stand up, gauging everyone's reactions. Garrett flinches, Nancy takes a sip from her wine glass, Juliette leans back in her chair, and my dad stands up straighter, watching me.

Mayson watches with rapt attention, not backing down. It's like she's waiting to see if I'm going to drag her into this. I look from her, to Garrett, then back to my dad.

"You're right, they would make a 'great pair.'" I swear I hear Mayson gasp in surprise, but I'm not done. "Then when she's unsatisfied in bed because he doesn't know what he's doing, she can go find a real man to fuck on the side. What a happily ever after."

There's various sounds of shock around the table as I walk away, even with my dad calling my name I don't turn around. I swear I hear footsteps, but they aren't heavy like his. When I hear Juliette call out for her daughter I know it's her.

I get outside, and go to open my car door when I'm pushed from behind, and turn around to see Mayson shaking her head at me.

"You're such a dick, you can't help yourself can you?"

"No, I can't," I sneer.

"You don't own me. You don't have any say about me or my life."

"So you've said, but we both know that's not true. Don't worry, those people in there are too stupid to think I was talking about us."

"I wouldn't be too sure about that," she huffs.

"Come with me then." I nod to the car.

"Where are you going?"

"Anywhere that isn't here."

I see her hesitate. "When are you coming back?"

"When I feel like it."

She looks back at the house, then back to the car. "Don't make me regret it."

To my surprise, she jumps in with me. I take off before anyone comes outside, without a plan in place, but I know where we can go for some distraction.

I END up taking us to one of my old practice fields. The area is lit up from some dim lights around the area. I go to the trunk to grab a ball I have back there, and it's a little deflated, but it will work. I toss it up in the air, catching it in my palm as I close the trunk and look over at her. "You want to play me?"

She looks at me skeptically. "I don't think that would be a very fair game."

"I'll take it easy on you."

"Oh, I meant it wouldn't be fair for you." She smirks.

I nod. "Let's see what you got then, Dunne."

I toss the ball at her chest, and she catches it easily, examining it. "This ball is flat."

"It's good enough. We don't even have a goalie, you can handle a little less air in the ball."

"Sounds like you're trying to cheat." She looks at me skeptically.

"How?"

"I'm not sure yet, but I'll bet you are."

I shrug. "Play me and find out."

Mayson tosses the ball up in the air, seeming to think about it. "Fine, but don't let me win. I want it fair."

I bark out a loud laugh. "I would never *let* anyone win. Not even you."

"Good. I just want to make sure that when I beat you, you can't use that as an excuse." She drops the ball down, and immediately starts dribbling it around me before I have a chance to register that we've even started.

I turn around to chase after her as she kicks the ball toward the goal I guess we silently decided was mine. When I try to steal the ball away from her, she manages to keep it away, and I can't help but be

Then, I cheat. Wrapping an arm around her middle, pulling her into me as we tumble to the ground. My chest shakes with laughter, but Mayson lets out a growl, smacking my leg before rolling off of me.

"That's cheating. This isn't football," she scolds.

"A lot of other countries actually call it football."

"Well we aren't playing tackle football." She stands up, wiping the grass off her ass, even though I doubt there's any there.

"Lighten up." I join her in standing, bending down to grab the ball once again. "You cheated first, then I did the same."

"It's always tit for tat with you, isn't it?"

I shrug. "Sure, if that's what you think. Fine, no cheating."

Rolling my eyes, I reluctantly agree because all I want to do is tackle her to the ground again, but this time, I'd make sure to pin her there and make her scream.

We get in position for kick off and I do my best not to cheat as we play one-on-one. Of course I can't help it some of the time. I do end up with the first goal which has Mayson pouting in a way that has me wanting to push her down onto her knees and feed my cock inside that plush mouth of hers.

"Again," she demands and I smirk at her determination.

Mayson's playing is borderline violent, but little does she know I like it this way. It's practically foreplay for us, kicking the ball back and forth, bodies getting close while we try to steal it from each other. It takes all my effort not to tackle her onto the turf again.

She manages to score on me, and does the cutest little victory dance. "Not so big and bad, are you?"

I scoff, "We're tied."

"I still scored on you." She folds her arms across her chest, standing tall with her chin up.

"Next one that scores wins," I state.

"If I win, I get to move back into my dorm."

I laugh. "Your empty dorm? Last I checked you don't have a roommate anymore."

"Even better. I get the place to myself."

"Not going to happen, but nice try." I shake my head. "Plus last I checked, you've seemed to like the new living situation."

She grimaces. "I wouldn't go *that* far."

"You at least like to be around me, admit it."

She moves the ball between her feet. "Yeah, no, I'd rather we get back to the game."

"Fine, but you're not moving out." We get back onto kick off position when I continue. "Oh, and you aren't going out with that piece of shit back at the house, either."

"I think I missed the memo of when you had any say in what I get to do."

I crowd her, collaring her throat to hold her against me. "You're right, you did. It was when I was buried deep inside you that first time and you were too busy screaming my name to notice anything else."

She slaps my cheek, the bite of pain makes me laugh. I tighten my grip on her throat. "That was cute. Next time, try a little harder."

I let go, and she sways where she stands, which I take full advantage of. She recovers quickly, and we fight for possession of the ball. Just when I think I'll get a good shot, she manages to get the ball away from me. And I do the same to her, it actually turns out to be harder than some of the actual games I've played.

Finally, I'm racing toward the goal, kicking it in, and without a goalie, it soars in easily.

I turn back toward Mayson with a smile on my face. "I win."

CHAPTER 28
MAYSON

I'm fully prepared to get reamed by my mom once Colin and I get back to the house. Luckily, it looks like Garrett and Nancy are gone. I try to sneak upstairs, keeping close to Colin like his large body is going to hide me, but I swear my mom has some sort of sixth sense and calls out for me.

We get to the top of the stairs, and Colin pushes me in front of him, hiding me even more as my mom's voice gets closer calling my name once again.

"Mayson, get down here."

I freeze. Colin slides his hand onto my hip, then to my stomach, pulling me into him. "You can talk in the morning, it's been a long day," he speaks up.

"Colin, honey, no offense, but I need to talk to my daughter. Alone."

I feel him tense behind me. I sigh before telling him, "It's fine."

"I'm joining you," he growls against my ear, but I shake my head.

"No, you're not."

"Mayson, come here." My mom's tone is more irritated, and Colin tenses even more.

I break away from his hold, turning to face her and don't miss the grimace she lets out at my appearance. My hair is in a messy ponytail, sweat slicked and I know I have dirt on my clothes from our impromptu game.

Without letting it affect me, I climb down the stairs while I feel Colin's anger radiating off him. I know he wants to be involved in everything that has to do with me. But unless he's about to tell my mom what we've been up to then he's going to have to back off. Though, I wouldn't put it past him to blurt it all out right here without a thought.

I'm surprised he doesn't say anything else. In fact, I hear him walk toward his room as I reach my mom at the bottom of the stairs.

"What were you two doing?" she sneers.

"Playing soccer." I fold my arms across my chest.

She looks up to where Colin just disappeared from, and nods in the other direction to the kitchen. "We need to talk."

When I go to sit on one of the stools at the counter she stops me. "You are not getting the chairs all dirty."

I roll my eyes. "The maids Walter pays good money for can clean them because we both know it wouldn't be you."

She gasps, "What happened to you? Where did my sweet girl go?"

I furrow my brows at her. "What're you talking about?" I don't think I've ever described myself as sweet, and neither has she.

"Is this because of Colin? He's rubbing off on you, isn't he?"

I suck my bottom lip between my teeth to prevent myself from saying how he's definitely rubbing *something* on me.

"Honestly Mayson, this was supposed to be a fresh start for us, but all you've done is fight me at every turn. Then, you disappear with Colin coming back looking like you were mud wrestling."

I look down at myself, seeing dirt smudges, but I think she's being pretty dramatic comparing it to mud wrestling.

"We played some soccer, mom. I was bored out of my mind here with your friend."

"Well, it was rude. And you're going out with Garrett."

I curl my lip in disgust. "I really don't want to."

"Too bad. It's already happening. Saturday before you head back to school."

"I'll leave before then."

"Honestly, Mayson, why must you fight me on everything?"

"Because I don't want to go out with him, and you're trying to force me."

"Are you seeing someone else? Is that it?"

I open my mouth, then close it because I don't have a good response to that.

"That's what I thought." She nods before I can even say anything. "I expect to see you *clean* in the morning."

She dismisses me. I grumble, walking away knowing the conversation can't lead anywhere good if I continue to fight with her. Instead, I head upstairs quickly toward my old room, but I'm pulled through a different door, and yelp as it's closed behind me.

Colin crowds me against the wood. "What did she say?"

I scoff. "Like you weren't listening."

"Fine, I was, and you're not going out with him. I already told you that."

I roll my eyes. "Yeah, well you heard me try to get out of it already."

"No one gets to touch you, but me."

"So you've said," I deadpan. "Let me go so I can take a shower and go to bed."

"Shower with me."

I shove at his chest. "Can I not have five minutes alone?"

"Nope."

I groan, pushing him hard enough I get some space. "I'm showering and I'm going to bed. *Alone.*"

To my surprise, he lets me have the distance, but that smirk on his face makes me feel like it's going to be short lived.

"Fine, have the night, babe. Tomorrow is a new day, and seeing you walking around this house knowing what you taste like is going to make it a lot harder for me to stay away."

"Well you better try because tomorrow is Thanksgiving and you're not going to get me alone all day."

He lets out a low laugh. "Watch me."

I love how she thinks I won't get her alone. I love how she thinks I wouldn't tell everyone I know what my step-sister feels like. What she looks like when she's lost in pleasure, and what she tastes like when she floods my tongue with her cum.

She clearly doesn't know how far I would go to let the world know she's mine.

She also doesn't realize how desperate I am for her again because it's been too long, and not having her in my bed last night is only making me more determined to have her today.

Especially when I catch her going into the pantry in the morning, probably looking for her oatmeal. She's reaching up trying to get the container off the top shelf. There's no way she can reach without help when I step inside the small room, closing the door behind me. But there's no lock.

Mayson whips around to glare at me. "Why do you keep doing this?"

"Doing what?" I step closer to her.

"Locking us in rooms together."

I look back at the door handle, then back to her. "There's no lock on this door."

"It's a figure of speech." She rolls her eyes, and I push her up against the shelves, causing her to gasp.

"I know what it is."

"Great, let me leave before we're caught."

I chuckle, running my finger up her thigh, grazing the hem of her sleep shorts. "Get caught doing what? Standing here?"

She swallows roughly. "Standing *closely*."

"Is it illegal to stand close to someone?"

"No, but..."

"But what?" My hand moves higher up to her hip.

"But you're touching me."

"I could touch you more."

"Don't."

I raise an eyebrow, hooking my index finger in her shorts, seeing if she's actually going to stop me, but she doesn't. Her hand slaps down on my bare chest, fingers sliding down the indents of my abs. She traces the V that girls are obsessed with, and I'm not about to interrupt her exploration. Even as I start to pull down her shorts and her eyes shoot up to mine, her hand remains on me.

"Why not? You're touching me," I tease, moving her shorts further down off her hips.

"I just don't know what else to do with my hands," she whispers.

"Right. Well, how about if I lift you up, then you can use them to pull on my chain you love so much while I fuck you."

Mayson scoffs, "You're not fucking me in here, you psycho."

The challenge spurs me on, pushing her shorts all the way off, stepping on them so when I hoist her up in my arms they stay on the ground while she wraps her legs around my waist and I push up against the shelved wall. Shit falls on the ground, but I don't even pay attention to any of it because her bare hot cunt is pressed against my stomach. My hips jut forward out of pure instinct as she grabs onto my shoulder, digging her nails into my skin.

"I'm not?"

She shakes her head, but at the same time she moves so her heels are trying to push down my sweatpants.

I chuckle. "You sure about that?"

"I don't think I'm sure about anything when it comes to you."

I help her get my pants down over my ass, freeing my erection, angling to rub it through the wetness between her thighs, but not pushing inside her yet.

"Then tell me you want it. Tell me you want my dick inside you, Mace."

She whimpers, moving her hands to the back of my neck holding onto me there. "Fuck me, but you better make it fast."

"Why's that?" I'm barely holding on by a thread.

"Because we don't have a lot of time before someone catches us."

I pull back, then push inside her with a single thrust that has her gasping against my mouth as I drop my lips against hers, but refuse to kiss her.

"Then I guess you better stay quiet." I pull back before pushing in roughly once again. "But I want to make you scream."

I slam my mouth down onto hers in a brutal kiss, needing to feel more of her as her pussy squeezes around me. I love how she kisses me like she hates me. Maybe she thinks she does. But with the way she's bouncing on my dick while I fuck her against the shelves it sure doesn't feel like it.

"Scream for me, babe, let mommy and daddy hear how much you love coming on my cock."

She shakes her head, fighting the urge to cry out. While I'd rather not get interrupted, I would love to see the reaction our parents would have at finding out what we've been doing while we're alone. Am I fucked in the head? Yes. Do I care? Not even a little bit.

I reach between us, finding her clit to rub while fucking her so hard her back must be digging into the wood behind her. She doesn't complain or try to stop me other than trying to drag my mouth back down to hers to muffle her gasps and whimpers.

"Who makes you feel this good?" I ask when I feel her tighten even more around me, and I'm fighting the urge to come.

"You," she moans.

"And who am I?" I push, mostly because it bothers her.

"Colin," she moves, trying to meet my thrusts with her own as I pick up speed.

"Who am I *to you?*"

"My stepbrother," she gasps, and I can tell how close she is. Which only makes me fuck her harder. She gets off on how sick I am too. How sick we *both* are.

"That's right I am. And I'm going to fill up your pretty little cunt, and you're going to have to go the rest of the day with our family knowing you're full of your stepbrother's cum."

I crash our mouths together, forcing my tongue between her lips, while I swallow down every noise she makes as her entire body tightens as her orgasm racks through her. I grip her hips even harder as she squeezes my dick so tightly I practically see stars as my own release takes over. I push into her as far as possible to make sure I fulfill my promise of filling her up.

I'm somehow going to go the entire day with this secret

between us. I don't know how I will refrain from dropping down to my knees at the dinner table to have her for dessert.

Well, I guess I will, but maybe I'll wait until we're back in my bedroom.

Which may be even more difficult if she keeps looking at me like she is right now. Pupils blown, lips red and swollen, knowing her pussy is the same. I flex my hips, pushing in even more to force the cum even deeper inside her.

"Mayson?" The shrill voice of her mom calls out. When she stiffens in my arms. I just smirk.

She tries to wiggle out of my grip, but I keep her pinned, even when her mom calls out again, this time she sounds closer.

"Let me go," Mayson whispers.

"You want to go out there right now?" I look down at where we're still connected. "Like this?"

"It's better than her *finding* us." She tries to get me to put her down, but I keep her pinned in place.

"She'll leave."

"Colin," she growls my name in the cutest way.

"Yeah, baby deer?"

Her eyes narrow at me, knowing how much she hates her nickname.

"Mayson!" her mom calls out again, but she sounds further away now.

I set her down, and she immediately reaches down to snatch up her shorts. She slaps them against my leg before pulling them on. "That's not fair you know?"

"What isn't?" I smirk, pulling up my own pants once again.

"The stupid thigh tattoo, the chain." She waves her hand around. "All of it."

"Just say I'm hot. It won't kill you." I rest my hand against a shelf, leaning on it and towering over her.

"I think it actually might," she grumbles, fixing her clothes and patting down her hair, but it was already messed up even before we did anything.

"Why? I think you're hot." I shrug.

"Oh do you?" Her hands are on her hips and she's giving me a disbelieving look.

"No shit."

"Interesting, because I remember what you said the first time you saw me, and it was definitely *not* because you found me attractive."

"What did I say?" I try to recall that first day because all I remember was being pissed off that my dad was forcing me to move back in. And then even more mad that I was about to share a house with this girl I didn't know and couldn't touch.

"I'll let you think on it." She pats my chest before pushing past me and leaving the tiny room we've been in. The cool air from the rest of the house sweeps in as I watch her leave.

This is going to be an interesting holiday.

CHAPTER 30
MAYSON

You know what's worse than sitting at a Thanksgiving table with your weird dysfunctional non-family? Sitting at said table with said people *and* the guy your mom is trying to hook you up with. While next to your stepbrother who fucked you into oblivion earlier.

Add in the fact that I can still feel his cum dripping out of me. Everything is such a mess.

Colin's anger is palpable but no one else seems to notice. Maybe Garrett does because he's sweating bullets and it doesn't make a date with him any more appealing.

"Pass that to me, would ya, Gary?" Colin grunts and I watch Garrett look around, hesitating before he speaks up.

"Pass you wh-what?"

Colin glares instead of saying anything else, and I roll my eyes at the weird show of dominance going on right now.

"Colin, don't be a dick," Walter scolds before taking a hearty sip from his drink.

"How am I being a dick?" Colin's gaze finds mine from

across the table where I'm seated next to Garrett. I know it's pissing him off even more that he can't touch me right now.

But I'm sure he's more than happy to know that I can still feel his cum leaking out of me. Just thinking about it again has me shifting in my seat and I know Colin notices. The smirk on that stupid face makes it obvious.

"Mayson, why don't you tell Garrett about what you're up to at school," my mom encourages for some reason.

Oh, you mean what I do in between the time when I'm riding my stepbrothers dick in the house I was forced to move into with him?

"Yeah, Mayson," Colin chimes in like he always does. "Why don't you tell *everyone* what you're up to at school."

I wonder if he can read my mind because between his tone and the way he's looking at me, it really feels like he's in my head in more ways than one.

"Just playing a lot of soccer," I mumble before shoveling a giant bite of food in my mouth to keep from saying anything else.

"That's not all she does," my mom tells Garrett and Nancy. "Mayson is extremely smart, she's going to be a fantastic doctor."

"Physical therapist," I grumble with my mouth still stuffed full of food.

"Don't talk with your mouth full," she snaps.

"Yeah, Mace, don't talk with your mouth full." Colin winks and I narrow my eyes at him.

"Anyway, yes. My daughter is going to be extremely successful. Smart and gorgeous. She's perfect." My mom is laying it on *thick.*

"You putting her in the show pen, next?" Colin snarks.

"Excuse me?" my mom gasps.

"Just saying, you're selling her like she's some prized animal up for auction."

"Colin, that's enough," Walter snaps to his son who's just sitting there proud of himself. And pissed off.

But what else is new.

"Want to list off all my accomplishments for everyone, then dad? How much do you think you could sell me off for?"

"Watch it," Walter threatens, and it reminds me so much of his son, it's almost scary.

"Anyway, you two will have such a great time." My mom directs her attention back to Garrett while I watch Colin stab his fork aggressively into a thick piece of turkey.

I don't say anything else, but I know one thing is for sure. I will not be having a good time with the guy sitting next to me. Not just because of Colin, but because my mom isn't about to control my life like that.

I hate to admit Colin being right about something. But with the way she's selling me to this man and his mom, she's being pretty obvious. I will date whoever the fuck I want to. Colin aside, if I want to be with another man or woman I will. And there's nothing any of them can do about it.

SOMEHOW WE MANAGE to get through the extremely awkward dinner mostly unscathed. My mom tries, once again, to push Garrett and me together to talk, though I have nothing to say to him. I'm also pretty sure he's too scared to say anything to me.

That night I'm lying in bed scrolling through my phone when a text pops up.

BLAKE

Are you alive?

MAYSON

Somewhat. Colin is going to send me to an early grave.

BLAKE

I feel that. Especially when the British Bastard was driving me insane.

MAYSON

Was Mads really that bad?

BLAKE

Yes. But I cured him.

MAYSON

Guess I'm the only one hoping I'll be left alone after all of this is over, huh?

BLAKE

Or get your happy ever after *wink emoji*

MAYSON

Don't get sappy on me, now.

BLAKE

No promises.

I chuckle, but I know there will be no happy ending for us. I also know Colin will never leave me alone, I'm stuck with the miserable asshole for the foreseeable future. That's even truer when my bedroom door swings open, and said miserable asshole enters quickly, locking the door behind him.

I sit up, glaring at him as I fold my arms across my chest. "What do you want?"

"To leave. Get your shit."

"Why?"

"Because I'm fucking sick of being here and watching your

mom try to set you up with that limp dick. I want you back in my bed and I'm not waiting until the weekend is over to get it."

I want to argue, but I also want out of here just as badly.

For the first time I think ever, I listen to him willingly. Packing up my stuff once again and sneaking out of the house to head back to the one I've been seeing as a prison. But really it seems like it's a sanctuary compared to this one.

I don't fight at all as we get into the car and drive back toward Seattle.

Even though the drive is short I end up dozing off. I'm currently jostled awake when Colin scoops me up out of the car. I squirm in his arms. "Put me down."

"No."

I don't fight very hard as he carries me inside, not even bothering to turn on any lights. I don't even think he got our bags out of the car. For a brief second I think he's going to take me to my own room. Of course he doesn't, and instead is dropping me roughly on his mattress, making sure I'm awake.

"Wha—" I start to ask what his problem is, but he's ripping off my sleep shorts, then climbs on the bed, between my legs laying on his stomach. He moves my legs to rest on his shoulders, my heels digging into his back and then his mouth is on me.

He's running his tongue along my slit and I buck up against him.

"I couldn't wait another fucking second to taste you," he growls before sucking my clit into his mouth so hard I cry out.

My fingers sink into his hair, yanking the strands and holding him right where I want him to be. His tongue flicks the sensitive bundle of nerves so rapidly I swear my vibrator could never compete with what he's doing to me. I pull his hair even harder when he shoves his tongue inside me and licks me so completely I think I may have an out of body experience.

"Fuck yeah," he groans. "Cry for me as you come. I want to hear you."

And I do, pulling at his hair even harder as I cry out, my orgasm taking over completely. It feels like it goes on forever as he works me through it. I hardly notice when he moves to hover over me until his mouth is on mine and I'm tasting myself on his lips. I suck on his tongue, savoring the mixture of us.

I reach down to palm him through his shorts, but he takes my hand away and pins it next to my head. I let out a small whine, hooking my leg around his waist, and pulling him down onto me to silently demand what I want.

"Aw, you want to be fucked?" he mumbles against my lips.

I nod, trying to rub myself up against him.

He chuckles, rolling onto his back, and taking me with him. "Cute. Go to sleep."

"What? No. You want me to ask you for it and then when I do you deny me? Are you actually mentally okay?"

He hums, settling deeper into bed, and keeping me close with a tight grip around me. "Probably not."

I huff out a breath, but somehow end up drifting off to sleep.

CHAPTER 31
COLIN

When I wake up, Mayson is still passed the fuck out, so I decide to go to the gym for a little bit. Maybe I'll be nice and bring her home a coffee from her favorite place. Right before I make sure to feed her my cock for breakfast. I wanted to drive her crazy last night by not fucking her, but damn did that take some self control.

My phone rings as I finish up a set and when I look at the screen to see my dad's name, I debate throwing it across the room to make sure it shatters.

Then I would have to get a new one and make sure it's set up to track Mayson. That sounds like too much of a pain in the ass to deal with. My dad calls again, and this time I answer gruffly, "What do you want?"

"Where did you take Mayson?"

"Back home. We were done being there."

"Bring her back. You can leave if you want, but her mom wants her here."

"That sucks. She doesn't want to come back and last I checked, she's an adult." I add more weight to the bar,

170

knowing I'm going to need to let some aggression out after this phone call.

"Colin, don't be difficult."

"Send a car to bring her back since you just said it yourself, you don't care if I join."

I don't give a fuck that he doesn't want me there. I'd rather take a soccer ball to the nuts than go back over there. Especially with Mayson only to watch her mom try to sell her like cattle to some limp dicked asshole to marry her off.

"She won't come back without you. Do you think I'm blind or just stupid?"

"Definitely stupid, but your eyesight is probably going in your old age."

"You're not as smart as you think you are, Colin. You're going to ruin her fucking life if you continue what you're doing."

"And what is it I'm doing?"

He scoffs. "You've had it out for that girl ever since she moved in. I'm sure it's just because you can't have her, that's why you wanted her so bad. But it needs to stop."

"Last I checked you guys were the ones that wanted her to move into the townhouse with me. What was the reason again? To *protect her?*" He acts like he wasn't completely on board with the idea when Mayson's mom pushed it. And now she's pushing her daughter to another man.

"I thought maybe I could trust you not to *fuck your step-sister*, but I suppose I was asking too much of you."

"Yeah, I guess you were." I don't bother to deny it. No matter what he thinks is going to happen, he's going to have to get used to the idea sooner or later.

I'm not giving her up, it doesn't matter what anyone says, including her.

"Bring her back, or I'll cut you off. Goodbye soccer, goodbye school, goodbye to your party pad."

I laugh. "Yeah? You do that then there's really nothing stopping Mayson and I from running away somewhere and never returning."

"You don't call the shots, son. I do."

"We'll see about that."

I hang up before he has a chance to. I'm not about to call his bluff because I know that's exactly what it is. He thinks he controls my life, and maybe in a way he does. But I also know that he's not going to piss off his precious wife by cutting off Mayson.

And I'm not giving her up either.

With that in mind, I get back to working out until my muscles ache.

By the time I get home, Mayson is still sleeping. I can't help but look at her, taking in that soft exposed skin. I revel in it. How it tastes, how she looks when she's lost in her pleasure. How she fights me, but gives in every time. *How she's all mine.*

AFTER THE HOLIDAY BREAK, we're all back at it with practice and some of the guys clearly slacked over the four day break and are slower than they were before. I want to call them out on it, but I'm not Doc or the captain. I do look toward Mads to see if he'll say something, but his mind seems to be somewhere else.

Not exactly what you want in a goalie and I kind of want to toss a ball at his head. I refrain, but only because Vito and Reyes are saying some shit about the Rites.

"You're not even fucking around with it since you have a girlfriend...supposedly." I roll my eyes. I still don't believe

Reyes is actually dating this chick, even if he wants everyone to believe it.

"Yeah? And what're you doing other than fucking your stepsister?" He retorts.

"Trust me, she's still my target. Some of us didn't puss out on tradition."

Vito scoffs. "Yeah, and some of us take it too far, but you're fucking goldilocks doing it just right, huh, Masters?"

"Bite me, DeVito." I use his whole last name instead of his nickname.

"Where do ya want my teeth?" He bares them at me, and I just roll my eyes at the pair of idiots I happen to be forced to share a team with.

After practice, we're all back in the locker room and I'm tossing my shit inside. Then I think about how I told Mayson what she has to do while living with me. And that I haven't been hard enough on her, despite what she may think. While we've had our fun, I have yet to forget how she was going to go out with that guy her mom was trying to set her up with.

How she still doesn't believe she's mine.

That needs to change.

Now.

I grab all my shit from my locker, tossing it in my gym bag to bring home.

"Get together at my place later tonight. Show up if you want," I announce to my team. It's time, Mayson sees that she's mine and everyone else is going to see it as well.

When I get home, Mayson isn't here yet. I go directly to her room, and dump the contents of my gym bag on her bed, smirking at the thought of how mad she's going to be to come in here to see my sweat covered clothes all over her clean sheets.

173

I leave the mess as I go to my bathroom to take a shower, hoping it's where she'll find me when she comes home.

The screech I hear as I'm rinsing my hair has a smile spreading on my lips, seconds before the shower curtain is ripped open. Revealing a little pissed off woman.

"What is your fucking deal?" she snaps.

"You haven't been carrying your weight around here. I had some laundry that needed to be done." I run my hands down my face to wipe off the soap that fell from my hair.

"Oh I haven't? Making sure your cock is drained every fucking day isn't enough for you?"

"Nah, that's just a bonus." I wink, reaching down and giving said cock a quick tug, which draws her attention down to my thickening length. "We had a deal. I gave you your clothes back to be nice, but I can be mean again if I need to be, baby deer."

"Stop calling me that." She grimaces. "And you never stopped being mean you asshole."

"Yes I have, and I can remind you what it was like again." I grab my towel off the hook, wrapping it around my waist, and walking past her to my closet. I don't even turn around when I continue, "Some teammates are coming over later."

"Let me guess? I need to be locked in my room again like your fucking prisoner?"

"No, you can join this time." I turn around to face her. "You can see what it feels like."

"What?"

I don't answer, getting dressed and ignoring her again. My mind filled with the thoughts of what my dad said about not having her. Thinking of her mom trying to set her up with someone else. Someone that isn't me.

I'm not going to let her go, I never could, but I want her to see what it's like to think I have. For her to see how badly she wants me. To prove to herself that she won't let me go either. And that it will always be us. It was always going to be us.

CHAPTER 32
MAYSON

I need a fucking hazmat suit to walk into my own room with the sweat soaked clothes that have officially ruined my bed. I don't even want to go near them, let alone touch them to move them anywhere.

Colin's always keeping me on my toes, but I feel like I've officially gotten whiplash. He wants me, but he also wants to drive me crazy. He wants to lock me away in my tower so no one can see me, but he wants me to be around for the party tonight. He challenges me to date that Garrett guy, but whisks me away from the situation.

Then there's the fact that he yanks me into his bed every night and fucks me until I can't breathe. But the next morning we go our separate ways. We aren't a couple. We aren't admitting any feelings. We're just fuck buddies...I guess?

Then why does the thought of that make my stomach cramp? I hate myself for the tinge of pain because that makes me feel like my heart is becoming involved and I refuse for that to be true. I can't fall for Colin, regardless of him being my stepbrother or not. It's because it's *him*.

I don't know what he has planned for tonight, but whatever it is I'm sure I'm not going to like it. And whatever ends up happening I'm sure somehow, someway I'm going to end up in his bed.

I can hate myself later for it.

I end up gathering my comforter up, balling Colin's nasty clothes in it so I don't have to touch them. Of course, I don't throw them in the laundry when I bring them down to the washer. I dump them on the floor, and toss my oversized blanket in the machine. He can deal with his own shit because I'm not his maid.

His bedroom door is still closed when I head back to my room, and I wish I could lock myself in here. I also think about how funny it would be if I were able to lock him out of his own party.

Now there's an idea for another time.

I text my team group chat telling them to come over because if the guy's team is going to be here, I'm not about to face them all alone. Plus having my friends around makes it easier to deal with Colin and his bullshit.

As I'm getting ready I hear voices downstairs, and I know the chaos is about to begin. I pull my long hair up in a ponytail, not because I know it drives Colin crazy. Nope. It has nothing to do with him at all.

Liar.

"Are you decent?" a familiar female voice asks from the cracked door.

"Would you care if I wasn't?"

Anja bursts in. "Nope."

She's followed by Maeghen, Chelsey, Blake, and Lucy.

"Do you know how hard it is to find outfits that go with *green hair?*" Lucy flops onto my bed in annoyance.

"You can pull off anything and you know it." I roll my eyes

because she could have any hair color, or no hair at all, and would still be gorgeous. She's just mad the color wasn't her choice.

"Yeah, well I got him back so it was worth it." She smiles.

"I'm really glad Luca has gone easy on me." Chelsey shakes her head and we all glare at her.

"Some of us definitely haven't gotten it easy," Blake grumbles and I nod in agreement.

"Do you know the reason for the impromptu party?" Maeghen asks and I just shake my head.

"Does Colin ever need a reason? Other than to piss me off?"

"Oh yeah, I'm sure that's what he's been doing, right?" Anja gives me a look.

"Yeah, what else would he be doing?"

"Uh, fucking you senseless?" She chuckles, and everyone mumbles in agreement.

"Oh please, like you all haven't had sex with someone you didn't like before?"

They all pause before murmuring agreements.

"Besides, it doesn't matter. I'm just using him to get through these next few months. Then the Rites will be over, the season will be done, he'll graduate, and that's it."

"That's my girl." Anja raises her hand up for a high-five. "Hit it and quit it."

I chuckle. "No shit. It's *Colin*. It was never going to go anywhere."

Yet when I say the words, the stupid pang in my stomach is back and maybe I need to see a doctor about it. Because there has to be something medically wrong. In no way does it have to do with anything else I may or may not be feeling for Colin.

Because I'm not feeling anything other than disdain.

I can't.

B<small>LAKE BROUGHT</small> a flask full of vodka that we've all shared while we hang out in my room before heading downstairs. As the music gets louder and more voices appear we decide we should probably join.

That, and we ran out of our own alcohol.

Downstairs, I don't immediately see Colin and vow not to seek him out. I'm sure his eyes are going to be on me even though I don't want them there. I stick close to my friends as we navigate the crowd of people that have overtaken my house.

Mads is quick to steal Blake away, and she doesn't immediately call out for help so I figure she's okay with it. I want to get out of the stuffy house, and step out into the backyard. The cool air instantly feels so much nicer, but then I see him.

"Oh shit," Maeghen says, seeing what I am.

Colin is in the hot tub, but of course he's not alone. He's shirtless with only that fucking chain around his neck. The one I've had bite into his skin while we've had sex. Right now some girl I don't recognize is toying with it while she's talking to him. Of course it's not just them, there are several women in the hot tub, and they're all looking at him like they're about to know what it feels like when he's holding them down and fucking them.

What he does to me.

Every night.

Yet, right now he doesn't even see me or the fury I'm sure is evident on my face.

"Want to kill him?" Maeghen asks, and I shake my head.

"No. He just wants to get a reaction from me." I know that's what this is, but I can't help the way I do want to kill him.

Every time he's gotten mad another man has looked at me. Every time he's gotten mad at me for talking to another man.

And this is what he's doing?

Fuck. That.

I walk over, doing my best to hide any emotion, keeping my head held high as I approach.

"How's the water?" I ask no one in particular.

The girl playing with Colin's chain gives me a disgusted look. "We're full."

I smirk. "Looks like it."

"Nah, we have room for one more, babe." He pats his lap. "Right here."

"Darn, you know I would love to, but someone has taken away all my swimsuits."

"You don't need them, we're all friends here."

I see the girl narrow her eyes at me.

"Friends? Is that what we are?" I ask my stepbrother.

"What else would we be?" He lifts an eyebrow.

"I would never consider you a friend," I sneer.

"Come on, Colin. Let's just get out of here." The girl tries to entice him, but he isn't even paying attention to her.

"Yeah, Colin, why don't you get out of here? I can find plenty of fun for myself for the night."

His jaw clenches, and I know he doesn't like the thought of that. *Good.*

I start to walk away, but I hear splashing, and then a very strong, very wet body is behind me, pulling me back against him and I'm lifted off my feet.

"Let me go," I screech, trying to fight him off, but he doesn't.

Instead, he carries me into the hot tub, fully submerging me with him and I try to push away because my clothes are now completely soaked.

Some of the girls get out of the water, making sure to loudly express how annoyed they are. But when Colin turns me around in his lap, his eyes are blazing. I try to push at his shoulders, but he's not letting me go.

"I would never consider you a friend either." His mouth crashes onto mine. I almost forget where we are and the amount of people around. The way he's kissing me is so intense everything else seems to fade away.

It doesn't seem real, especially when I give into it, kissing him back. My fingers sink into his hair, and pull the strands roughly causing him to groan. His hands grip my hips, and pull me onto him so I'm straddling his lap. Our lips don't part from each other. Colin's tongue invades my mouth as he pulls me even harder against him. I can feel how hard he is against me, even through my soaked pants.

"Um what the fuck?" A snarky voice sounds from somewhere close by. I break away from Colin's lips, but he just moves to run them along my neck, nipping the skin and then soothing it with his tongue.

"I think the message is pretty clear. You can leave," I tell the girl that's still sitting in the water for some reason.

"Aren't you like siblings?"

Colin lifts his head, his hand on my ass is keeping me completely plastered against him. "Yeah, we are, so you should probably leave so we can have some family bonding time."

I laugh, even though I shouldn't. He's so sick, and it's wrong. But dammit watching the snarky bitch's face curl in disgust as she has to climb out of the hot tub embarrassingly makes it worth it.

"You're gross," I tell him, our lips less than an inch apart.

"You like it." His mouth is on mine again, and dammit, I do like it.

CHAPTER 33

COLIN

I don't give a fuck who is watching us right now, what they think or who they're going to tell. My team's known Mayson is mine for years, even though she didn't know it. Now the entire fucking school can know and I don't care. What's surprising is that she's letting this happen. I fully expected her to try to pull away, maybe slap me or something that would only turn me on more.

But this is better. Her grinding on my lap while kissing me in front of everyone. Yeah, this is my girl. I just wish she wasn't wearing as many clothes, but then everyone else would see her, and that's something I don't want.

We need to move this to my room because I need her naked. I need to feel her. I fucking *need* her. I didn't think it was possible to need a person this much, and that's how it's always been with Mayson. I crave her in more ways than just one. I crave her body, but I crave her fight, her back talking me, her drive. It's just *her*.

"Fuck, let's go," I groan, lifting her up out of the water because I think she's about to make me come if we keep this up much longer. And when I do I need to be buried deep inside her, not grinding against her in a hot tub.

Mayson is sopping wet as I set her on the ground, before jumping out to join her. I wrap my arm around her shoulder and lead her inside. I catch a glimpse of Reyes sulking in a corner, probably on his way to being shit faced. He's been off for a little and I don't see his supposed girlfriend around.

I still don't believe that fucker was dating anyone, but who am I to say. The only person that deserves an ounce of my attention is currently shivering next to me as we quickly head upstairs. No one pays us much attention, not when there're so many people around and the music is blaring. Even if they are, they can stare and say whatever they want.

As soon as we're in my room, I guide her into the bathroom, noticing how she hasn't fought me since she got in the hot tub with me. I'm about to ask if she's feeling okay, but then I'm too distracted by the fact that she's pulling off her soaking clothes.

"Guess I ruined your plans for the night," she sasses, stepping out of her pants.

"Nah, you just made them better." I cross my arms over my bare chest.

"Yeah? How's that?"

"How'd it feel?" I divert.

"Which part?" She pulls her shirt off over her head, and I'm too distracted by all her bare skin to say much. I see the goosebumps appear as the cool air hits her already chilled skin.

"All of it," I grunt, already forgetting what we're talking about.

"Seeing you with those girls? Having your tongue in my mouth in front of them? Which part?"

"Yeah." I clench my fist to stop myself from grabbing her right now.

"Didn't matter to me. I knew no matter what you'd come to me begging to fuck me when you got bored with your games." She shrugs like she means it, but I can sense the lie.

It got to her. She didn't like it and she was *jealous.*

I chuckle. "That's cute. You came to me."

"So?"

"So, you *wanted* everyone to see us."

"And?"

I smirk. "Now you know what it's like to have someone trying to take you away from me."

She steps closer, her bare chest barely grazing mine. "No one is trying to take me away now. So, what're you going to do about it?"

I snap, pulling her into me, grabbing the back of her neck. I bury my hand in her hair, yanking the strands to pull her head back, angling her right where I want her as our mouths come together like magnets. I pull her flush against me, her chilled skin against mine shocks my system like electricity buzzing beneath the surface.

I break our mouths apart, pulling her hair back roughly and she moans. "You want me to tell you what I'm going to do about it?"

Mayson bites her bottom lip, and nods, but winces at the bite of pain of trying to move her head.

"Or do you want me to show you?"

Her cold hand lands on my abs, sliding down to the waistband of my swim shorts, hooking her index finger in them and then pushing down. "Show me," she whispers.

I flip her around roughly, pushing her against the vanity, pinning her hips with mine. I love seeing her mouth drop in a gasp in the mirror as I cover her back with my chest, working my shorts the rest of the way down. I wrap my hand around my cock, squeezing it in my fist because I've been so hard for awhile now I feel like I could blow the second I'm inside her if I'm not careful.

I reach around to slide my hand down her stomach, and lower to find how wet she is. All while keeping my eyes on hers in the mirror.

"So wet for me, baby deer," I taunt.

"Don't call me—" She's cut off with a gasp as I shove a finger inside her roughly. She's soaked, already coating my hand as my palm rubs her clit.

She slams her hand on the mirror in front of us as she tries to rub herself against my hand.

"I'm the only man that'll ever touch you like this, and guess what?" I press my lips against her ear.

"What?" she breathes.

"You're the only woman I'll touch like this because you're *mine*." I press in another finger, curling them to find that spot that will make her knees buckle. "And I'm *yours*."

She cries out, trying to work herself against my hand even harder. I rub her until she's right on the edge, so close she's tightening around my fingers and her cries get louder. I pull away, moving my arousal covered fingers up to her mouth, pushing them in so she's forced to taste herself.

Mayson moans around them, sucking and licking the taste of her from my skin, and I about lose it. I angle myself against her entrance and push in roughly. She squeals with my fingers still in her mouth and I drop my mouth to her shoulder, my teeth sinking into her skin as I bury my cock so deep inside the tightest, wettest channel. I fight off the impending orgasm until I can fuck her thoroughly through at least two of her own.

"This is how you always should be," I groan against her, removing my fingers from her mouth to grip her throat and make sure she keeps her eyes on us in the mirror.

"Struggling to stand?" she sasses.

I chuckle darkly, tightening my grip on her neck and slapping my other hand down on the side of her ass. "Naked and filled with my cock."

"That doesn't," she gasps when I pull out and thrust in again, "seem practical."

"I don't give a fuck if it's practical or not." I pull almost all the way out, kneading her ass, then letting spit from my mouth fall between her cheeks before I push back in roughly.

She moans so loudly I know everyone downstairs could hear if the music wasn't so loud. I rub against her tight hole, pressing my thumb there and she bucks back, so I press down between her shoulder blades to hold her in place as I slam forward again.

"How's it feel, babe?"

"A lot," she whimpers.

"Good, but you can take more."

I pull back, thrusting into her once again and she lurches forward, planting both hands on the glass in front of us.

"Eyes up. Don't look away." I demand, holding myself deep inside her, waiting until her tear filled eyes look into mine through the mirror. "So fucking pretty."

I slam forward again, and I don't let up. Fucking her as she meets me thrust for thrust. When I put pressure against her ass once again she tightens even more around me.

"You like this don't you? Want to be my dirty little slut? But only for me. Only for your *stepbrother.*"

That does her in, crying out with release as she strangles my cock as she comes. I hold back, just barely, and I feel her arousal coating me, dripping between us. When she comes down, I reach around to rub her clit to get another one out of her as I continue to fuck into her roughly. I'm fighting off my own orgasm, doing everything I can to keep it at bay until she's whining that she can't take any more while also coming once again with a shrill cry.

I'm unable to hold back any longer. My thrusts increasing as I come with a groan, biting her shoulder as the orgasm racks through me. I fill her, making sure to push in to get my cum in her as deep as possible.

We don't move right away. We're both breathing heavily, and I finally lift off her back, looking down to where we're still connected. I keep a hand on her back to hold her in place as I pull out. When my cum starts to drip from her I push it back in and she moans, lurching forward.

"Colin," she whines.

"Hm?"

"I'm sensitive."

"I know, and you're going to walk like the cute little baby deer you are again." I smirk when she makes a small growling noise that's more like a baby lion. "But all is right in the world because you're full of my cum again."

"I think I'm always full of your cum," she grumbles, standing up straight as I lift my hand off her.

"That's exactly how you fucking should be."

"You're a caveman," she scoffs.

"Yeah, but I'm *your* caveman."

She makes a face that's a mix between annoyance, and a smile. Yeah, I'm hers and now everyone knows it too. I don't even give a fuck about the shit I'm about to get for it. Though, I should probably be worried about the backlash of being caught shoving my tongue in my stepsister's mouth, I couldn't give less of a shit.

It's finally time the rest of the world knows Mayson Dunne is mine and always has been.

CHAPTER 34
MAYSON

After practice, I look at my phone to see I have a missed call from my mom. It only causes me to roll my eyes and toss it down while I change out of my gross uniform. The same one I'm thinking of leaving on Colin's bed as revenge like he did to me.

"So are we going to talk about the other night?" Anja speaks up.

"What about it?" I shrug.

"The whole...ya know." She turns around, wrapping her arms around herself and acts like she's making out with someone.

A few of my teammates laugh, and I can't help but join in as I toss a towel at her. She turns back around with a big smile on her face.

"You really are getting the ultimate revenge for the Rites, aren't you?" Lucy nudges my arm.

"What do you mean?"

"Getting him to think you're into him. Playing the perfect little hostage. I'm sure he loves it, and then when the season is over you can *rip it all away.*" She laughs almost manically and the rest of my team that's paying attention joins in, all calling me a genius.

I forgot I told them that was my plan the other night and join in with agreeing that I have the greatest plan. I don't like lying to them, I didn't when I initially said it and I don't like it now. But it gives them an explanation for why I would make out with Colin where everyone could see.

And then fuck him where no one could.

"How are you going to do it? Publicly in front of his team?" Chelsey sounds giddy at the thought.

"I haven't decided yet." I shrug as I finish getting dressed.

"I think the guys have been having a rough season anyway, them losing a bunch of their games may be amplified by some solid public humiliation." Maeghen shrugs.

I can't argue with that, from what I know Colin has been pretty pissed about the lack of wins they've had. Of course he always has someone to blame, and it's never his fault.

I say goodbye to my team, and as I'm walking back home I glance at my phone again to see the missed call from my mom has turned into several more missed calls and I sigh, dialing her back.

"Mayson, what on Earth have you been doing that you've been ignoring me?"

"Uh, school? Soccer?" I'm already annoyed at the conversation and it's barely even started.

"Why did you leave after Thanksgiving?"

"You're just asking about this now?" I pull my phone back to double check the date because I'm pretty sure it's been a week, but maybe I've teleported to some alternate reality and the last week has been a hallucination.

"Walter talked to Colin. I thought maybe your brother talked to you, and that you'd reach out."

189

I grimace. "Do not call him that, we are *not* related."

"You're family, but that's neither here nor there. I gave Garrett your number so you could still go on your date."

"Mom, you think I have time to date? I have too much going on as it is."

"Temporary things. I know you think you want to be a therapist or whatever, but Mayson you don't have to if you marry the right man."

"Physical therapist, glad you pay attention. And my life goal is not to marry for money, mother."

"I don't understand *why*. I gave you good looks, might as well use them."

I'm almost back to the house, and wanting to be off this phone call more than anything.

"Well, mom, you may not realize this, but I'm more than just my looks. I'm smart, athletic, and an all around good person."

"Of course I know that, which is why you deserve the best, and to not have to struggle like we did for so long."

"We were fine," I grumble, looking up at the townhouse I'm sharing with Colin. The modern architecture, the location so close to campus in Seattle, I know this place had to cost a ton of money. It makes me hate it even more. Something about the fact that my mom thinks money is the end all be all when we got by with far less. But then there's people like Colin and Walter who have more money than they know what to do with and it doesn't make them good people.

"Well now we're even better. Think about it, Mayson. You can't hide behind Colin forever."

"I don't," I scoff.

"No, but he thinks he has some hold over you. Walter is concerned. Maybe some space would be good for you two."

I bark out a laugh. "Oh now you want us to have space. It's a little late for that."

The front door opens, and there stands my overly attractive stepbrother. He must have been expecting me because what he's wearing should be a crime. The shorts he has on are short enough to show the viper tattoo wrapped around his thigh. The cut off shirt he has on is completely open on the sides. He leans against the door frame with his arms folded and eyebrows raised.

"Just think about it. And go out with Garrett. Even if he's not the one it's good for you to get out there."

"You know what," I say loud enough for Colin to hear as well. "I'm done with you, or anyone else telling me what I'm doing with my life. You can support me and what I choose to do with my life, or you can stay out of it."

I hear her start to argue, but I hang up, done with the conversation.

Colin doesn't say anything to me until I'm about to walk past him through the door. "That was hot."

"Fuck off." I push past him, storming into the house, done with everyone.

"That was even hotter." He follows me into the kitchen.

"I'm not in the mood for whatever you're planning or thinking, or just *you*." I wave him off as I grab a water bottle from the fridge.

Colin leans over the counter, just looking amused. "Who were you talking to?"

I take a large gulp of water before answering, and he just waits. That stupid look remains on his face. "My mom."

"What did she want?"

"What do you think?" I roll my eyes.

"They must be working together or something because my dad gave me shit about us recently, too."

"He knows?" I exclaim.

"He *thinks* he knows." He shrugs like it's not a big deal.

"Thinks he knows *what?*"

"Hold on, we can revisit that after you tell me what your supposed plan is with me." Again, he continues to look smug as shit, and my brain is moving a million miles an hour trying to keep up between the phone call with my mom, his dad knowing something, and now whatever it is he's talking about.

"What? Can we stick to one fucking conversation?"

"No, the other shit doesn't matter right now. I'm curious about what you're telling your teammates."

"None of your business," I scoff, moving past him because I need take five minutes to untangle my mind.

"See, it is my business because one of my teammates overheard you say something about using me until the Rites are over and that's it?" He doesn't look as amused now. He looks scary with that look in his eyes that has me straightening my spine and preparing for a confrontation.

"And? You believe them?" I sass.

"Should I believe you?"

"You can do whatever you want. I don't give a shit."

"But you should. And if you're not going to tell me, then you should run."

"Why would I do that?"

"Because if you're not going to tell me willingly, then I'll get it out of you." He pulls out that mask from Halloween from behind him, and starts slipping it on.

The sight instantly brings back memories of that night, and the slickness between my thighs intensifies because I'm depraved.

"What if I tell you?"

"Better do it quick, my patience has just about run out."

CHAPTER 35
COLIN

I pull the mask down on my face and watch as Mayson stiffens. Her hand tightens around the water bottle and I hear it crinkle as I wait to see if she'll say anything. Tell me it's a lie, that she isn't using me. Tell me that what's going on between us is real because I know it is.

But my team can't think I'm being played. You'd think the show we put on in the hot tub would set them straight. Or maybe they should see me fuck her just once. That would be enough to prove it I'm sure.

But they'll never see her like that. And she still hasn't said anything. If she's not going to say it, then her mouth can be busy doing other things. First, I'll need to catch her.

As soon as I move, she takes off running. She could go anywhere; up to her room, or to mine where she could lock the door herself. But she doesn't. She goes for the front door, and that just shows she really wants to play. So do I.

She races outside, and I follow, giving her a small chance to get away. She can think she'll be able to run and hide. She won't, but she can think it. I watch her head toward the trees, following a similar path from Halloween. I was more covered that day, and tonight the winter air has hit. The cold breeze assaulting my bare chest as I run only fuels me.

Once I've chased her past the tree line it gets darker than the lit street, and I utilize the sound of her footsteps crunching leaves as she runs. I watch her go behind a tree, and decide that this ends now.

"Baby deer," I call out, stalking toward her slowly. "Are you ready to tell me?"

Leaves crunch under my shoes, but she doesn't say anything. She also doesn't run again. I hear her loud breathing as I get closer to the other side of the tree. I'm fully expecting her to run again, especially when a stick cracks under my foot less than a yard from where she's hiding.

I move quickly, rounding the tree trunk, and caging her in against it. Even in the dark, her eyes blow wide as she starts to scream, but I clamp a hand over her mouth.

"You don't want to do that," I growl. "I'll take my hand away, and it's your last chance to tell me the truth before I force it out of you."

I slide my hand away, slowly, pulling her bottom lip down as I do. Her chest is rising and falling rapidly as she struggles to catch her breath. She doesn't scream again, but she also doesn't start talking either.

I chuckle darkly, shaking my head. "On your knees."

Her face scrunches, clearly not expecting that, but I don't care what she's expecting. This is what she deserves. I grab a fistful of her hair, and push her down to her knees, stepping closer so she's trapped between me and the bark behind her.

"Take my cock out. If you're not going to talk then you can choke."

She grabs the waistband of my shorts, and I really expected

more of a fight from her, but she pulls them down, freeing my dick from the confines as it bobs in front of her face. Without a single moment of hesitation she's wrapped her delicate hand around me, pumping. I pull on her hair, yanking her toward me.

"Suck," I demand.

Her jaw drops open, and she sticks her tongue out as I slide my cock onto it and into her mouth.

"Keep your eyes on me," I demand, thrusting forward, burying myself in her throat. "Tap if it's too much, and touch that needy little pussy of yours."

She gags and tears form in her eyes, but they stay on me like the good fucking girl she can be for me. She slides her hand into her shorts, doing as I say. I groan, keeping my fingers buried in her hair as I fuck her mouth. I expect her to tap, but she doesn't. Her nails dig into my thighs, but eyes remain locked on mine. The only part of my face she can see through the mask.

"You want to pretend like you don't want this? Want to pretend that everything between us is fake?" I grind out. She moans around me, the vibration feels way too fucking good. My release is so close, but I fight it, pulling her off.

She gasps for breath, panting while drool dribbles out of her mouth, looking like the prettiest fucking mess. And she's not backing down. The tears that streaming down her cheek aren't from sadness, her eyes are filled with so much need and fire, I tuck myself back into my pants and drop down to my knees in front of her.

Her eyebrows pull together and I pull the mask off, dropping it onto the ground so she can really see me.

"Tell me you've just been pretending this whole time."

She closes her mouth, and I hear her teeth click together.

I grab her face, squeezing her cheeks together. "Tell me."

"I—" she struggles, and I let up on my grip to let her speak. "I lied."

"Lied to who?" I narrow my eyes, feeling like she's about to continue to lie to me.

"To my teammates," she practically whispers.

"Because you like this. You want this, right?"

She nods.

"You want *me?*"

She nods again.

"Not some limp dick your mom wants to set you up with. Not because you're here for the Rites. You want me?"

Mayson scoffs. "I mean I wouldn't go that far, I still am only here because of the Ri—"

I cut her off, scooping her up in my arms and tossing her over my shoulder while she protests. I land a sharp smack onto her ass. She doesn't try to fight me too much as I carry her back to the house, and out of the cold.

Once we're inside, I'm salivating for more of her, and I know I can't wait to get her to my room. I drop her onto the kitchen counter, and she squeals when her ass hits the stone. I cage her in with my hands framing her hips.

"Since we're coming clean, I'll tell you everything too." She shifts around, breaking our eye contact, but I don't let her. Hooking my finger under her chin, I force her eyes up to mine. "But you're not allowed to let it change anything."

"That's not how this works," she argues.

"It is with us."

She looks at me skeptically. "I have every right to be mad at you if I want."

"Fine, you can be mad, but I'll always make it better. So when I tell you that I spiked your drink that night the Rites started to get you here, you can be mad, but not for long."

"What?" she screeches, slapping me and trying to push me away.

"It's not like I touched you or anything. I wanted you willing and able when that happened." I pin her legs down with my hips, and grab her wrists, locking them behind her back. "Which you were."

"You're fucking deranged. Get away from me."

"No, I'm not done with my truths yet."

"I don't give a shit to hear anymore from you."

"Too bad, you're going to." I hold her in place as I continue. "I knew you were going to be mine the second I laid eyes on you, and I wasn't going to stop until that was the case."

She scoffs. "You have a weird way of showing it. I remember when you fucked my friend my senior year."

"I wanted you to see. I wanted to see what you would do. I hoped you'd fight me. I've always loved your fight. I've loved everything about you."

"You wouldn't know love if it punched you in the nuts."

"What makes you think that?" I tilt my head in question.

"Well, we can start with the fact I think you might be a psychopath."

I shrug, waiting to see if she'll continue.

"You don't treat someone you claim to love the way you've treated me. You don't drug them, hold them hostage, lock them in their room, chase them through the woods, or do half the shit you've done to me."

"That's where you're wrong." I lean closer, keeping her trapped with my body. "My love may not be the sweet romantic bullshit kind you see in movies or read about in books, but mine is real. It's messy, chaotic, and yeah maybe a bit psychotic. But that doesn't mean it's not love."

"Maybe I want the sweet romantic bullshit."

I huff out a small laugh. "No you don't. Because you're

meant for me, which means my type of love is exactly what you want. More than that, it's the type of love you *need*. And I'm going to show you exactly how I know that's the truth."

I drop down to my knees, pulling her pants off quickly before throwing her legs over my shoulders and diving between them. Because while she may not admit that she loves me yet, we both know that's the case. It's only a matter of time, and until then I'll have fun pulling everything else from her until she finally admits it.

CHAPTER 36
MAYSON

I want to be mad at him. I really *should* be mad at him, he fucking admitted to drugging me. He's a deranged psycho that forced his way into my bed. But more than that, he forced his way into my heart, too. Somehow, some fucking way. Though, he did more than just force it. He bulldozed right past every wall I had up and made himself right at home.

Just like he's seemed to have made himself right at home between my legs with his face buried there while he makes me see stars. I've always heard about guys not wanting to go down on girls, or that they aren't very good at it. But not Colin. Of course the asshole is good at it. He's good at everything he seems to stick his mind to.

Which is probably why he was able to get me to feel things for him, even despite knowing what he did to me. Despite everything, my heart can't bear the thought of not being with him. Which probably makes me just as deranged as him, if not more.

That's exactly how I feel with the way he's able to easily

pull a powerful orgasm from me, and I go boneless at the sensations taking over me.

When he rises, his mouth and chin are coated in my release, and I whimper at the sight. Especially when he licks his bottom lip for more of the taste. I practically melt right off the counter at the indecent sight.

"Are you still mad at me?" he taunts, like he can read my mind.

"Yes."

"Guess I have to work harder for your forgiveness."

I try to push him away again as he scoops me back up. "You can't just win me over with sex."

"I can't?" he taunts, carrying me upstairs. "Seems like it's helping a little bit."

"Nah, I'm just using you some more."

He jostles me and I grunt as my stomach lands on his shoulder, knocking the air out of me.

"That's not as funny as you think it is." He slaps his hand on my ass and I let out a little growl in annoyance.

"I'm not trying to be funny."

"Good because we would need to work on your comedic skills if you were."

"Yeah, well we need to work on your romantic skills."

That earns me a laugh. "Now, that's funny."

I'm tossed down onto his bed roughly, and then he's on top of me, pinning me with his hips. His eyes are locked on mine. The dark blue is blazing while his hard cock is digging into me, making me squirm.

"What if I apologize? Would that make it better?" he asks. His deep voice seems even deeper, but I don't know if it's just my mind altering everything as lust consumes me.

"Not if you're doing it just so I'll let you fuck me."

"If you're upset about it, then I'm sorry. I did what I had to in order to get you here. I needed you close to me. Fuck the Rites, fuck all the bullshit that goes along with them. They were an excuse to get you close."

I scrunch my face at his half apology.

"You *drugged me*."

"And I'm sorry about that part, but I'm not sorry you're here. I'm not sorry about anything else between us because I know you've liked it. I push, you pull. It's how we are and it only proves how you've been mine for longer than you realize."

"No," I deny.

"No?"

"No. That doesn't prove how long I've been yours."

"You don't think so?"

"No. It proves how long *you've* been *mine*."

I wrap my arms around his neck, pulling his face down to mine so I can kiss him with all the aggression, and emotion I'm feeling without having to say anything else. He groans against my mouth, especially when I wrap my leg around his hip, pulling him even tighter against me.

His tongue plunges into my mouth and I can taste myself on it, which only makes me arch up into him even more.

"I'm still mad. Fuck me like you hate me," I gasp.

"No." He thrusts against me just once and I want more. I *need* more. "I'm going to fuck you like I love you."

"That's a thin line for you," I retort weakly as his lips trail from my jaw, down my neck.

"My love for you isn't sweet, it isn't nice. It's brutal and you may think it's hate, but it's not. It never has been. It's us, and I know your love is the same." His teeth sink into my skin where my neck meets my shoulder and I claw at his back.

He's pushing my shirt up, over my head, then latching his mouth onto my nipple, biting and sucking roughly. I can't say anything back because there's nothing to say. He's brutal, and he may be right. That's how his love is.

And the worst part is he may be right that my love may be the same. Because the fire burning in my chest, the ache that's there when I've thought about not being with him, are pretty telling. But my head hasn't caught up yet, since it's turning to mush with every second he's touching me.

He moves to my other nipple, sucking even harder than he did on the first one, and I cry out.

"It was always going to be me. No one else could give you what you need. No one else could love you the way you need, baby deer."

Nodding, because I don't know what he wants me to say. I just need him to fuck me before I lose my mind.

I push his shorts off with my feet, and feel his huff of laughter against my skin, but it doesn't last long. I manage to get them low enough that I feel his bare cock against me. I buck up to rub against him, and it puts the tip of his raging erection at my entrance.

"Tell me how badly you want me," he grinds out.

I whine, trying to push him inside instead of saying anything, but he won't move.

"Tell me, and then you can ride my cock the rest of the night. It's yours."

"I want you, please, Colin. Please."

"That's my girl," he buries himself to the hilt in a single hard thrust. I cry out, but the stretch hardly even phases me. I'm so turned on that the only thing I can think of is how good it feels. And how it's not going to take very long for him to pull another orgasm from me.

"Yeah, I am," I admit softly as he pulls out almost all the way, but I wrap my legs around him tightly, yanking him back into me.

"Oh fuck, Mace," he groans, and I smirk, knowing I've gotten to him. Even just a little bit.

I may not have been actually using him, but knowing his weakness is *me* is the greatest information he could've given me. I know he's obsessed, he's been obvious about that. But it's confirmed that no matter what, he wants me.

He thinks he loves me.

I moan when he hits a particularly sensitive spot inside me, and I hate that my mind thinks maybe I could love him too.

I should be mad. I shouldn't ever forgive him for half the things he's done to me. But I feel like I could make him pay for the rest of his life. The life I could be in. The life I don't think he will give me a choice but to be in.

For some reason that's the thought that has my release even closer. I tighten my grip around him, digging my nails into his back as he fucks me. Our moans mix together along with the sounds of slapping of skin. The crude sounds only add to my pleasure as he builds the pressure inside me so much that I'm coming, unable to hold back my screams of pleasure.

Colin groans, barely holding himself up over me as he finds his own orgasm, pushing all the way in and filling me with his release. I do something I never expected to do, I tighten my legs around him, holding him deep inside me as he does.

Our chests are sticky with sweat as we catch our breaths, and I feel like I should hate myself right now. I should question everything that just happened, especially knowing the extent of Colin's insanity.

But the only thought I have is that I don't want to move. I don't want things to go back to how they were before. I want this, and worst of all is I want the man that's currently borderline suffocating me. I want him more than just physically. I want to be able to give him my heart.

It's only a matter of time before I do just that.

CHAPTER 37
COLIN

We've hardly moved, I haven't wanted to stop touching Mayson because I feel like if I let go of her, she'll run away and never come back to me. I wasn't lying. I know I love her, and it's the type of love that not everyone will understand, but it's ours. I know she doesn't understand it yet. I've had years to come to terms with how I feel. I've also always known how I am. She's still figuring herself out, and that's okay. I'm not going anywhere, even if she tries to get me to.

Mayson's fingers trail along my chest absentmindedly and I would've thought she would be asleep, but I know my girl. Her mind is moving a million miles an hour, and I want to know why.

"If you're still trying to fight what we're doing here you may as well give it up."

She huffs, but keeps moving her fingers along the indents of my abs, up my chest to my chain I always wear, knowing that she loves to fuck with it so much.

"My dad knows," I tell her.

"What!" she exclaims, sitting up suddenly.

"Sort of," I try to soothe her.

"Explain." She remains tense and I may have fucked up the one moment of peace we found ourselves in.

I groan, pulling her back down, and resting one of my arms around the back of my head. "After Thanksgiving he wanted me to bring you back to their house. He also basically said he knows how I feel about you."

Outwardly accused me of fucking her, which I didn't deny.

"And what did you say?"

I shrug. "Not much to say, but he did threaten to cut me off."

"That would suck for you."

"It would suck for you too."

"Not really. I wasn't born with a silver spoon in my mouth like you," she sneers.

"No, but you've benefitted since it's been put there." She starts to get up, already annoyed with me, but I hold her even tighter. "Don't be like that. I want you to benefit from my silver spoon. We can share it."

She scoffs. "I don't need your spoon."

"No, you don't, but you can have it anyway. You don't need to struggle again and I won't let him take it away just because he doesn't like us being together."

"I don't think that's up to you."

"It is," I insist. I have my ways. She doesn't need to know what those are yet, but I have them.

"My mom basically told me I need to marry for money and that none of my interests matter," she grumbles with her mouth against my chest.

I can't help but bark out a laugh. "Then she'll be really happy for you to marry me."

"Hold on, we aren't going that far." She tries to push away from me.

"No, not yet, but you will. One day."

"You're crazy."

I don't deny it, because I know I am. Obviously marriage is something in the future, but she hasn't even accepted loving me yet. We'll get there, one step at a time. Also, we have to deal with our parents first. As much as I don't want to go back home to see them again, I know it's going to need to be done.

Soccer used to be one of my favorite things to do. And generally it still is, but lately, I just end up pissed off at how shitty the team is this year. Reyes has been a mopey fuck and that's hardly helpful on the field.

Everyone else either seems to be too distracted or not giving a fuck to play well. It seems like I'm the only one able to handle the Rites and the actual sport we play. I also don't give a fuck about my classes, which takes something off my plate I guess. Some of these guys actually care about their grades and finals coming up.

Mayson does too, which is why for the last few days she's been a ball of stress. Between soccer, classes, and the anticipation of going home soon, she's been constantly stressed. I have then taken it upon myself to relieve her of that stress, which I know she appreciates.

Even if she doesn't say it.

Just like she hasn't said she loves me back, and that's fine. I'm not a words guy, I know she does even if she doesn't know it herself yet.

After another shitty game we lost, we're back in the locker room. Mads is grumbling to himself, which speaking of distraction, he has been as well. We've never chatted much so I don't give a fuck to know why.

Reyes is looking at his phone for the millionth time and tossing it down looking even sadder.

"How's the girlfriend?" I ask, knowing it'll probably piss him off.

"Don't fucking worry about it, Masters."

"I'm not. She'd have to be real for me to worry about anything," I goad.

He starts mumbling under his breath, and I don't think I've ever heard him be so quiet. I don't even really care to know what he's saying or what's going on with him. All I care about is that the team is shit, and he's part of the problem. So whatever is going on, he needs to figure it the fuck out.

Everyone does because it's post season and we won't get far. If we don't then I might have to start kicking their asses for subjecting me to such a shitty final college season.

Maybe that's why I couldn't be captain.

Whatever, it's not like Mads is doing the job well, the fucker is just as distracted as everyone else. I look over at him, finding him not paying attention to much around, and toss a towel at his head. He turns, scowling. "What the fuck is your problem?"

"My *fooking* problem is you're not keeping the team up to standards." I can't help but throw in a jab at his British accent. *What can I say, I'm just a dick.*

"Piss off, Masters," he spits, and because I'm in a mood after the loss I get in his face.

"No, if you're not going to whip these guys into shape, then I will." I shove him against the lockers, and he immediately reacts like I hoped he would, shoving me back.

"Masters, Keller, my office," Doc booms, turning around and just expecting us to follow her.

I shove Mads again for good measure, walking ahead to get the verbal ass beating I know is coming, which is fine. She's not going to kick me off the team or anything.

As soon as I walk through the door, our coach is standing behind her desk with her arms folded and glaring at me. "There a problem I should know about, gentlemen?"

I bite my tongue so hard I start to taste blood. I'm not scared of Doc, and I'm definitely not against talking back to her. But something like this I'd rather deal with Keller one on one not with our coach.

"No, Doc, tensions are just running high after the loss," Keller says and I roll my eyes. *Kiss ass.*

"Masters?" She raises an eyebrow at me.

"Yup, just some high tension."

She looks between us skeptically, but clearly doesn't want to deal with any more. She's already had enough bullshit to deal with the Rites going too far for some. I think the science lab is still looking for all the dead frogs that were stolen. I haven't heard anything being done with them, but I'm sure it's coming. Unless whoever took them gets caught first. Good thing I'm not involved in whatever the fuck that's about.

"I don't believe either of you, but also don't want to deal with anymore right now. Get out." We're dismissed, and don't stick around to push our luck any longer.

"You happy, Masters?" Mads bumps my shoulder as we walk out.

"Nah, but Mayson will make it all better. Maybe you need someone to help you not be a miserable fuck."

"Don't worry about me or my dick. We're both very happy."

"I'm not worried. Maybe you have a made up girlfriend like Reyes."

"Fuck off," Eli calls out, and I shrug.

"Maybe you can deal with your own shit instead of worrying about the rest of us." Mads tosses his shit back in his locker, and turns back toward me.

"My shit *is* handled."

"You sure about that?" he questions, but walks out before I can clarify what he means.

I'm sure he's just trying to fuck with me, but there's a voice in the back of my mind warning that maybe he knows something I don't.

I glance down at my phone to see a message from my dad, and my jaw clenches. It's almost like he's summoning us back home. I want to argue and fight it, but I'm also in the mood to fight.

I go home to see Mayson, and scoop her up. We have our parents to see.

CHAPTER 38
MAYSON

The drive to Mercer Island feels like déjà vu, especially since I wasn't able to prepare. Yet again, I'm being borderline kidnapped. I put up a fight since my team is going to the Championships and I really don't have the time between that and finals to be taking a trip home. I try to physically and mentally prepare, but I don't know what we're walking into as far as our parents are concerned. Or what they're going to have to say to us.

One thing I do know is somehow Colin and I are united in this. It's us against them, no matter what they try to say or do.

Rationally, I know I'm anything but rational and that I shouldn't have forgiven him for half the shit he's done to me, but somehow I have. I'm sure a therapist would have a field day with the two of us, but I'm choosing not to think about it too much.

All I know is that I like how it feels when we're together. Even when we're fighting and getting under each other's skin, it feels good. And weirdly it always has.

We get out of the car after parking at our parents' house.

Colin grabs my hand, but I yank it away. "What do you think you're doing?"

"I thought ripping the Band-Aid off would be best." He shrugs.

"I don't think walking in hand and hand like little kids is ripping any Band-Aid off."

"You're right. As soon as they see us, I'll stick my tongue down your throat."

I push him as he laughs harder than necessary at his own joke.

We walk inside, while I try to keep some distance between us. Colin does everything he can to stay as close to me as possible.

Luckily, as we walk in, neither of our parents seem to notice. Colin tries to yank me to his bedroom, but I fight him off.

I would rather hide, but we walk through the beautifully decorated house. There's a large ornate Christmas tree in the front living room, garland and lights covering various surfaces. You'd think my mom put in a lot of effort to make the place look this nice. But I know better, and that it was really someone she hired to do all of this.

"I think it's tacky," Colin comments at the tree, standing closer to me than he probably should, his chest covering my back.

I like him being this close, and I'm not going to move. In fact, I lean back against him, just to feel more of him.

"Just say you hate Christmas," I retort.

"Guess I'm just not a big holiday fan." His head lowers to my shoulder, resting his chin there as he speaks. "Except Halloween, that's become a new favorite of mine."

"Yeah?" I turn my head to the side, our lips barely an inch apart. "Why's that?"

"Something about a mask seems to get my girl going."

"That so?"

"Welcome home," my mom's voice calls out, and I jump away from Colin quickly, even though I can feel his annoyance instantly.

My mom and Walter are both walking into the living room where we're standing. I don't miss the look Walter gives his son. It's obvious what Colin told me before is true, and probably even more so now if he just saw even a second of how we were standing.

He knows.

I can't tell if my mom has any idea, but she's also always been a good actress. I think that's why she managed to land the perfect life she'd always dreamed of. Pretended like she fit in until she finally did.

"I feel like it's been so long." Mom pulls me into a hug that feels out of place. I narrow my eyes, and look over at Colin to see his reaction, but he's currently in a stare off with Walter apparently.

"Uh, it's only been like two weeks," I tell her.

"Well I know, but you left so abruptly I feel like we didn't get an actual goodbye."

"And again, it was only for a couple weeks. You've been on vacation longer than that before."

"Oh please, save the dramatics, Mayson," my mom scolds and I roll my eyes.

"I don't think I'm the one being dramatic," I mumble.

Neither Colin or his dad have said anything, but of course my mom grabs onto her husband's arm, drawing his attention away from his son. "Aren't you just so glad they're back, honey?"

"So glad. It's nice to have the whole family under one roof," Walter says, pointedly at Colin, who shifts on his feet.

"Yeah, nothing like being *close* with family." Colin wraps his arm around my shoulders and pulls me into his side.

I try to push away, but his grip is ironclad.

"That's the Christmas spirit." My mom says, even though Christmas is still weeks away. But she seems just as oblivious as she always is.

The tension is so thick, but clearly she's choosing to ignore it.

"Son, I'd like to speak with you for a few minutes, and we can let the girls catch up."

I shake my head because they act like we've gone off to war for months. Not back to the fancy townhouse paid for at our fancy college just across town for a two weeks.

"Fine," Colin agrees reluctantly, and I'm sure they're going to go to Walter's office for their 'chat.'

As soon as they're gone, the smile on my mom's face drops and she glares at me. "What's wrong with you?"

"What?" I rear back like she slapped me.

"I thought Walter was being ridiculous. When I told you I wanted you to be set up for life I *did not* mean with Colin."

Guess I was wrong, she does know.

"Why not?" I sass because if she knows, I'm not going to deny it.

"Because he's your brother, Mayson, what's wrong with you?"

"*Stepbrother*," I correct. "It's not like we grew up together, we were in high school when you guys got married."

"Still. He is not the one for you," she insists.

"Yeah?" I plant my hands on my hips. "And why not? If his dad is good enough for you, why wouldn't his son be good enough for me?"

I try not to cringe at my own statement, realizing how sick that sounds. But, a part of me relishes the taboo element of it all. I think back to what Colin said when he admitted he loves me. We're a better fit than I ever thought because no one else would be able to match my jagged edges with their own.

"I love Walter, but we all know how Colin is. That boy is not someone who would be able to give the life you deserve."

"What life is that? The kind you live with your fake, rich friends and your *super* amazing, *super* rich husband?" I scoff.

"One where you're happy. I don't know how this started or why, but it ends now. Walter is telling Colin the same thing. It's over for the two of you."

I glare at her even harder, biting my tongue. She may think that, but I have a feeling if that's what Walter is talking to his son about, he's not going to take it very well. I'm sure Colin will fight back. For the first time, I think we'll be fighting on the same side. Because instead of it being us against each other. It's us against them.

CHAPTER 39

COLIN

My dad walks ahead of me into his office, just knowing I'm going to follow. He may think I'm following because I'm listening to him, or that I care about whatever he wants to talk to me about. I shut the door behind me and stand against it with my arms folded across my chest. I'm not in here because I care what he has to say, or plan to give into whatever demands he's about to make.

"Sit down." He gestures to the chair on the other side of his desk.

"Nah, I'd rather stand for this."

He clenches his jaw before speaking again. "I see you're still playing with Mayson."

"That's not what it is."

"No? Isn't that how you are because I know I didn't raise a son that does relationships."

"That's because you didn't raise me at all." I shrug.

"I gave your mother all the money she asked for in raising you."

215

I roll my eyes, "Because money is the only thing that matters, right?"

"It is to you, because without *my* money, you lose school, soccer, and everything else."

I won't lose Mayson. It takes every ounce of will power I have to hold back from saying that to him.

"You wouldn't take that away, though," I push.

"I wouldn't?" he challenges, and I just shake my head.

"Nah. You won't."

"You want to test that?"

I shrug. "For one, I don't think you would cut Mayson off."

He tightens his jaw because we both know I'm right about that.

"You wouldn't want to ruin my chances of going pro and the bragging rights that go along with that so you can impress all your business buddies."

Again, his attempt at a non-reaction gives away how right I am.

"At the end of the day all you care about is your reputation, we all know this. And we all know cutting me off wouldn't look great for *you.*"

"What's your plan, then Colin? Because you marrying your stepsister wouldn't look great for any of us either."

I shrug again. "I don't care how I look, that's all you, Pops."

"What kind of life would you even give her?"

"Better than you gave my mom."

He barks out a laugh. "Oh please, your mom was set for life the second she got pregnant with you. I gave her everything she ever needed. And you, too."

"Trust me, I know. The checks you sent every month kept her more than happy, and she never gave a fuck about having me around. It just ensured the money kept coming."

"What? Do you want me to be sorry for that? I'm sorry

you've had everything you've ever wanted. Now that you can't have something, you want to be a spoiled fucking brat about it."

Now it's my turn to clench my draw. "You think that's all this is? I can't have her and want to piss you off?"

My dad just looks at me, and I scoff, starting to slowly pace. "You're unbelievable. What does her mom think?"

"She doesn't believe it, but I didn't show her."

My eyes narrow. "Show her what?"

He turns his computer screen toward me, and it's the view of the backyard at our townhouse, there's a bunch of people and when I see myself in the hot tub with Mayson on my lap I know exactly what night this is.

"You've been spying on me?" I accuse.

"I've been keeping an eye on *my* house to make sure my irresponsible son doesn't destroy it."

"Yeah, I'm sure that's what it is."

"If I had an issue with all the parties you throw, or anything else I've seen, you'd know about it. I've let you have unlimited freedom, but I draw the line here," he tells me, boldly.

"I wouldn't call it freedom, more like a fairly long leash."

"Dammit, Colin. I'm asking for this one thing and it's pretty simple. You to stop fucking around with your goddamn stepsister." He pounds his fist on his desk. It's probably supposed to intimidate me into complying, but it's not going to work.

"That's not going to happen," I state firmly for the last time before I bring out my own threats.

We glare at each other, neither of us having any intention of backing down on this.

"End it. I can handle the fallout of cutting you off, but the world finding out you two are together would be much worse."

I stand taller. "Where would the fallout of your own affairs rank on your fucked up scale?"

"What're you talking about?"

"You've always been a shit liar, I know you have a weakness for your secretaries, and I usually don't give a fuck. But you lay off who I'm with and I won't bring up who you're with."

I've had suspicions for awhile, but I don't have any concrete proof. Just the hope that he supposedly "loves" Mayson's mom enough to not obliterate another marriage because he likes to stick his dick in younger women on the side.

"I raised a real prick," he spits.

"Again, you didn't raise me at all." I don't let his words affect me, they haven't in a long time. "We're done here."

Without another word from either of us, I turn and leave his office, ready to have my girl back in my arms again.

By the time I get downstairs Mayson is in the living room with her mom, and they aren't alone. Her eyes shoot up to mine, wide with annoyance and probably a hint of fear for how I'm going to react. Because that woman from Thanksgiving and her dipshit son are here once again.

"You've got to be fucking kidding me," I groan. Mayson covers her laugh with a hand over her mouth while her mom turns and narrows her eyes at me.

My dad comes downstairs not long after me, and joins his wife on the loveseat she's sitting on. I shove myself in next to Mayson, not giving a fuck about the company around us. I stretch my arm around the back of the couch behind her. They're all lucky I don't pull her into my lap right here, right now.

"How were your finals?" Garrett asks. He's clearly talking to Mayson. I'm shocked and somewhat impressed he would actually try to talk to her. But of course I can't have that, so I answer first to draw attention to myself.

"Haven't happened yet, but I hardly study. I might just be naturally gifted with smarts and looks."

I hear Mayson scoff next to me.

"Uh, h-how's soccer going?" Garrett again asks Mayson.

"Ya know, my team isn't really playing up to my standards so I'm hoping I'll get them whipped back into shape."

"Colin," Juliette snaps with a forced smile on her face.

"Hm?" I pretend to act oblivious to what I'm doing, and I can feel Mayson holding back her laughter next to me.

"All due respect, sweetie, but I don't think Garrett is talking to you."

"Oh." I look back toward Garrett who almost looks like he's trying to use his mom next to him as a shield, and then back toward Juliette. "Well, with all due respect, I don't really give a fuck what Garrett is doing."

"Colin, a word," my dad says sternly.

"No, I'm good right here. And on that note, I don't think Mayson really gives a fuck about what Garrett has to say either, do you, *sis?*" I drop my arm onto her shoulder, pulling her against me.

She pushes at my side, but I don't let her go.

"Colin," my dad snaps again, and I ignore him.

"Tell me something, Garrett, do you even think you could handle a woman like this? She's a feisty one."

The guy sitting across from me gapes like a fish and it's so funny, it only spurs me on.

"Do you have any masks? I know she has a soft spot for them. Especially if she's being chased through the woods."

"Colin!" my dad tries again. Tensions in the room are increasing, and Mayson is digging her knuckles into my side, but I don't stop.

"Can't take it easy on this one. Think you can handle that? I'm not talking about just a little hair pulling and a light slap on the ass. She wants it to hurt."

"Colin, that's enough." My dad looks like he's about to burst a blood vessel and I really don't want to stop because Garrett looks like he's about to pass out. I feel like the idea of anything I've said is completely foreign to him.

I stand up, stretching my hand toward Mayson. She looks up at me, my silent request for her to make her decision. I can see her internal debate, the risk we're going to take if she puts her hand in mine.

But she does it anyway.

I pull her up, tucking her into my side, as we turn to leave this hellhole. "Oh, one more thing." I turn around.

"For fucks sake," Mayson mumbles.

I pull my chain from underneath my shirt. "She's really into this chain, likes to choke me with it. And something about thigh tattoos and guys in crop tops really get her going." I shrug adding fuel to the already lit fire.

"Are you done?" She shakes her head against me.

"Yeah, I think so." I lock gazes with my dad. "Remember what I said."

No one says anything as we walk out the front door.

CHAPTER 40
MAYSON

I haven't looked away from Colin the entire drive back to Northgate. I can't decide if he's lost the last little bit of his mind that I thought he may have still had. It's either that or I've lost mine for being so head over heels in love with him.

His hand has been resting on my thigh the entire drive, but neither of us have spoken. I just stare at him. His relaxed posture, with one arm extended onto his steering wheel, resting his wrist on it. His eyes are focused on the road ahead, the street lights illuminating his face every time we pass underneath them.

His lips are quirked up in a smirk, and I'm sure he's overly pleased with how he handled everything back there.

He pulls into the garage, and we're immediately surrounded in silence when he cuts the engine. His eyes swing over to me, the weight of his hand still on my thigh. Tensions feel at an all time high as we just sit here in deafening silence.

"What happens now?" I finally ask.

"Now? I think we can start with you going upstairs, getting naked, and waiting for me."

I roll my eyes. "That's not what I meant."

"Well, that's what I think happens now."

"I'm pretty sure you just got us cut off, so I'm more focused on that than you wanting to get your dick wet."

Colin chuckles, getting out of the car, and I don't follow right away. He comes out to the passenger side door, opening it and waiting for me to step out.

"Come on, I'll explain inside." I sigh, swinging my legs out, and standing. "After getting my dick wet."

I shove him. "No, you're explaining first, then *maybe* I'll fuck you."

"Oh baby deer." He pulls me against him tightly. "You're not going to be fucking me, that's my job."

I push away from him and he laughs as we walk inside separately. As soon as I get to the couch, I drop down onto it, and wait to hear his explanation. I need to know if I'm going to need to start packing my bags and trying to get my dorm back. Blake isn't there either and it wouldn't be the same without her, but I'll figure it out.

Living apart from Colin again would be an adjustment as well. One, I don't particularly want because I think I've been officially Stockholmed.

He joins me on the couch, pulling my legs into his lap before explaining. I tell him about my conversation with my mom, and he tells me about the one with his dad. Especially the threat he made about revealing Walter's affairs. It doesn't surprise me, even if it should. I can't help but laugh at the thought that my mom's "perfect" life she thinks she has really is flawed beyond repair.

"After your tantrum you threw, you really think he's not going to cut you off?" I question.

Colin shakes his head, pursing his lips, "Nah, he cares more about what your mom thinks than what we're doing. They'll get over it eventually."

"Will they?" I make my doubt known.

"Probably not, but it won't matter. I'll go pro after graduation, and neither of us need them."

I scoff. "You're really confident about that for a guy on a team that's on quite the losing streak."

"The team may be, but I'm not. I already have shit lined up."

I roll my eyes, my tone is sarcastic when I say, "Of course you do. Colin Masters always has everything all figured out."

He moves my legs off his lap, and within a second is over me, his body covering mine, playfully pinning me down. "Yeah, I do. Anyone who knows me, knows that when I'm the striker, I'm going to score."

"Oh my god," I groan mixing with my laughter, wiggling underneath him. "You're so ridiculous."

"Good thing you love it." He drops himself lower onto me, the pressure of his weight on top of me feels so good like it always does. His lips linger less than an inch over mine.

"Good thing I love you," I whisper, hooking my finger in his chain, and pulling hip lips down to mine in a vicious kiss.

It's brutal like it always is, his tongue invading my mouth, tasting every inch. He pulls back too soon, and I try to chase his lips with my own, but he remains hovered above me.

"Say it again." He smirks.

I try pulling him back down by his chain again, but he doesn't budge. I let out a frustrated growl that only makes him smile.

"Say it," he demands again.

"You may be crazy, fucked up, and wrong for me in more than a million ways, but I love you, Colin."

He groans, dropping his forehead down to mine again. "I fucking love you, Mayson, I'm glad you finally caught up."

His lips are on mine again, and this time neither of us stop. Neither of us slow down to let anything in the outside world distract from us. Our relationship may never be accepted, and we may lose the only family we have. But it wouldn't be much of a loss because we have each other.

Other people may not understand us, our relationship, our connection. But it doesn't matter because we do. We may not know what the future looks like for us, but I know one thing. I somehow, someway, fell in love with Colin Masters.

It's crazy to think how easy everything has been after we left our parents. No dealing with family, needing to put on a show to impress my mom or Walter. Just Colin and me, lost in each other for days on end.

It's like we created our own perfect world where it's just the two of us. I've been waiting for the other shoe to drop, to get an eviction notice or something on the door. Or that our tuition has been pulled, but none of those things happen.

Colin may have been right, and his threat to his dad worked. But neither of them have reached out to us either. I'm sure it's only a matter of time, but truly, they're the last thing on my mind.

Even school has been on the back burner because soccer has taken over almost completely. It may be finals time, but it's also the post season. And all my focus is on the championship.

The guys, not so much, and I've had to hear about every mistake Colin's team has been making almost every game. And then he takes his frustrations out on my body, which I will never complain about.

Of course the cocky bastard is right about the teams shitty performance not affecting his chances of going pro. Because he showed me his offers from a couple teams. He really is a good player, and his ego isn't entirely misplaced. Which only makes him more unbearable at times, but also only makes me love him even more at the same time.

I also benefit from him celebrating every time he gets an offer because he likes to take his good moods out on my body as well.

I do the same with every win my own team has, then coming home and using Colin as my own personal jungle gym. Which I know for a fact he doesn't mind either.

We're living in some sort of bubble I never expected to be in with the man I was convinced hated me from the moment we first met. Turns out there's a fine line between love and hate, especially with him. It also turns out we both like toeing that line and how it feels when we fight, and then how it feels even better when we make up.

The guy's team is out early in the postseason, but we're in the finals and it feels damn good. Even better, Colin gets to come cheer me on at my games. I know a lot of the guy's team has been coming to our games. It might have something to do with a couple of budding relationships that stemmed from the Rites. Even if it's not, it's definitely a way for us to shove the fact that we're better right in their faces.

My mom has never been one to come to my games, but something about this being the championship and knowing she's not going to be here feels like a final nail in the coffin of our strained relationship. It's always had issues, but she's made her choices.

And so have I.

I hate that I have one more year of school left, aside from grad school, but I'm hoping to get a scholarship so I don't have to deal with worrying about being under anyone's control. Including Colin. Despite what he says about doing whatever he can to help me, I don't want it. I don't want to rely on anyone other than myself.

"Who's ready to kick some ass?" Lucy calls out right before we're about to run out onto the field.

We all yell out, "Go Vipers!"

Then we're headed out onto the field. We get in position, and I can't help but look up into the stands where I catch sight of the entire men's soccer team in the stands, standing and cheering.

"They're trying to fuck," Anja jokes.

I chuckle. "Yeah, I think they are, actually."

"Good. I volunteer." She waves up at the stands and I laugh harder.

My eyes find Colin easily, and he winks at me. I volunteer too, but only for that one. The cocky, asshole striker. That one is mine.

CHAPTER 41

COLIN

There are few things that are hotter than watching my girl play soccer. Watching her ride my dick, watching her suck my dick, and watching how she comes. But seeing the way she dominates the field during a game, especially one as high stakes as this, has me rock hard and ready for her as soon as they secure this win.

Which I know they will because it's been a bloodbath. Literally since one of the Vipers gave one of the girls on the opponents team a bloody nose from a rogue elbow. Which did cause a penalty, but it hasn't hurt the Vipers chance at winning because the score is still three to one.

I hate not being out there, and I'm still mad at some of the guys sitting in the stands with me. Despite our shitty season, I still have a handful of teams up my ass about wanting to sign me. I guess I can't be too mad. If it had jeopardized my chances of going pro, we would've had a problem.

Mayson is going to be working on getting into grad school, so wherever I choose to sign I want to have a school for her to go to. If she thinks we're going to be apart, then I'm going to do everything to set her straight. She's mine, and now that she's accepted it herself she's not getting away.

The Vipers score another goal and we all cheer. The game only has five minutes left, and unless they completely fuck it up, they're going to secure the win.

Mads and I aren't even at each other's throats. Reyes hasn't been as much of a miserable fuck lately, even with us losing so I don't know what changed with him. Technically the Rites ended as soon as our season did, but it faded for a lot of the guys before then like it always does.

I'll never stop fucking with Mayson, and I know she feels the same. That's part of what makes us such a perfect match. We don't need some hazing ritual as an excuse. It's just us and always has been.

The clock on the game runs out, and the whole place loses it with excitement. We all lead the way, running onto the field.

I find Mayson immediately, she's sweaty, her ponytail is messier than when the game first started. She has dirt on her uniform and skin, and it only makes her even hotter to me. I snake an arm around her from behind, pulling her into me.

"Good game, baby deer."

She turns around with a wide smile on her face, tossing her arms around my neck, and I lift her easily into my arms as she wraps her legs around my waist.

"Can't really call me that since I'm able to walk, or run as you clearly saw," she teases.

"I'll call you that forever. Just like I'll always remember how you looked trying to walk after the first time we—"

She cuts me off with her mouth on mine, and I let out a laugh against it before kissing her back. Neither of us care about all the people around us, what they could be thinking or will say about us. None of it matters. My girl won her championship, and she's *mine*.

Even better, I get to take her home, and show her just how mine she is. All night. And maybe I can even convince her to stay in bed all day tomorrow. Or for the next week.

We break apart and Mayson wiggles in my arms. "Put me down, I'm a mess."

I grunt my refusal. "You know I like it when you're a mess."

"You like when I'm a mess from *you*."

"You're wrong. I love when you're a mess from me. But also I just love you."

She smiles, and it's almost giddy. "I love you too." I kiss her again, fully intending to take her out of here while she stays wrapped around me, but as I start to walk away, she fights in my arms. "Don't try to kidnap me yet."

"Why not?" I complain.

"Because we just won the championship and you have to share me."

"I'll never share you," I growl.

"Tonight you will, at least for a little bit." She manages to get down, but I keep her held against me. "After we get back home I'll make sure to make it all worth it."

"I know you will." I kiss her again, and then let her pull me into the crowd of people. I don't stray far from her, always having a hand on her in some way as the team celebrates.

Even as the celebration moves to our house, I don't get mad that we don't have alone time because I get to touch her all night. And she'll pay for making me wait. She always does.

THE NEXT MORNING I wake up the best way I've ever experienced. My cock enveloped in the tightest, wettest, warmest place I've ever felt. Mayson's hands are planted on my chest as she lifts up and drops back down. I grip her hips as I start to open my eyes to see the glorious view.

And *fuck* is it glorious.

She's naked, her perfect tits bouncing every time she impales herself on my cock. She throws her head back, her long dark hair falls down her back, and I want to wrap it around my fist so bad. But I also don't want to move and lose this sight.

"Couldn't even wait for me to wake up, could you?" I groan, digging my fingers into her hips.

"Your dick was awake enough for me," she gasps, lifting up and dropping back down again.

"It always is," I grind out, needing to control her pace a little longer or I'm going to come way sooner than either of us would like. "You woke up needy and desperate for me?"

"Mhm," she hums, grinding herself so her clit rubs against my pelvis in a way that drives her crazy.

"Fuck yeah, babe. You going to make yourself come like this?"

"Yes, I'm close. I need more," she whines.

"More? Tell me what you need."

Her nails dig into my pecs. "*More.*"

I scoot myself back on the bed, wrap an arm around her as I sit up so we're face to face. Then I do exactly what I wanted to, grabbing a fistful of her hair, and yanking her head back. At the same time I wrap my lips around one of her nipples and suck hard. She squeals at the simultaneous pressures. I thrust up into her and she cries out.

"This what you need?" I move to her other nipple, sinking my teeth into her flesh hard enough to have her yelping.

When I pull back from her chest, I bring her face to mine. "Come for me. Show me how tight you squeeze my cock with this perfect little cunt."

She screams with her release, tightening around me hard

enough I groan, thrusting up into her, chasing my own release that's impossible to hold back any longer.

I pull Mayson's mouth onto mine as my orgasm takes over, we aren't even kissing, just breathing each other's air as pleasure takes over. I bury myself deep inside her as I come for what feels like forever.

I seal my mouth over hers, kissing her like she's everything because she is. She's everything to me.

And I tell her exactly that.

"You're everything, Mace."

She huffs out a small laugh, pulling back to look at me with a smirk. "That's it?"

I let out a loud laugh at her using the same two words I said when I first saw her. I end up rolling her onto her back as she starts laughing. "Sounds like you need more," I tell her, already hard for her again, and make sure to thrust roughly.

This is exactly how I plan to spend the next several days. No interruptions, just us.

Of course that would be ruined not long after we both find releases for the second time. A door shuts downstairs, and we look at each other because we're usually really good at locking the door, and the only other person that has a key...

"Colin. Mayson. Get down here," my dad calls out. Mayson looks at me wide eyed, but I just shake my head.

"I'll handle it. You can stay here."

Quickly, I pull on some shorts, but don't bother with a shirt as I race downstairs and see my dad and Juliette standing in the living room. The place is still a mess from the party last night, and I can see Juliette's reaction is obvious by the disgusted look on her face. My dad is just glaring at me.

"Where's Mayson?" he snaps.

"Upstairs, I told her I'd handle you."

"I'm sure she'd like to see her mother." My dad gestures

toward his wife who is still looking around with her lip curled in disgust.

"I don't think so. You won't be staying long anyway," I state, folding my arms across my chest. "Especially because we both know you have nothing to say. Unless you want me to share what I know."

"That won't be necessary." He glares at me. "We're here because we wanted to tell you *both* something."

I clench my jaw. "Fine. I'll get her."

Without giving him a chance to say anything else I go upstairs, and see Mayson laying in my bed, scrolling on her phone. "They want to talk to both of us."

She groans, "So much for you handling it."

"I do have it handled," I grumble as she pulls on one of my T-shirts and pair of boxers.

"Sure seems like it," she comments sarcastically, walking past me out the door.

I roll my eyes and follow her downstairs, hoping that whatever is waiting for us isn't going to ruin the peace we've found ourselves in this morning.

CHAPTER 42
MAYSON

I woke up in a great mood, had some orgasms, just won a soccer championship. Everything is pretty fucking great. Until my mom showed up with Colin's dad to ruin it all. We haven't heard from them since we walked out of their house, and now they just show up here.

"What do you want?" I ask, wanting to get this over with.

"Mayson," my mom gasps in shock.

"What? You haven't talked tried to reach out, and now you just show up here? It must be for a good reason."

"Mayson, what is going on with you?" She places her hand on her chest, and I'm pretty sure she would clutch her pearls if she was wearing any right now.

"What's going on is that you want to control my life. You don't care about what makes me happy, but want to tell me what to do. Did you even know my team just won the championship yesterday?"

Her throat bobs on a swallow, and I know that's the answer I'm going to get.

"Yeah, didn't think so." I look at Walter, already fired up. "And you, are you going to make more threats to try and drive us apart? Because I'm going to tell you not to waste your breath."

"Mayson Anne!" my mom squeals. "That's enough."

I feel a warm hand on my waist, and Colin's large body behind me. "I actually don't think that's enough. Want to keep going, baby deer?"

"If you wanted more say in my life, maybe you should've actually been a mother instead of focusing on what you could get out of a man."

"That's not true," she gasps.

"No? Okay, sure." I roll my eyes.

"We came down here to tell you both that we don't accept what you're doing and we never will," Walter adds, and it only gets me fired up even more. Colin too, with the way he tenses behind me, but his dad continues. "But we've realized you both are adults and if you want to ruin your lives this way, then go ahead."

Colin scoffs loudly, "Funny how you think we're ruining our lives. I've never been happier."

"I bet." Walter glares at both of us.

"Did you come here with anything productive to say because it seems like the same shit we've already talked about," Colin goads.

"You're not being cut off." Walter seems to be pained in admitting that.

"Great, you can go then." Colin gestures toward the door.

"After you both graduate, you're on your own."

"Good. We don't need you," Colin insists, again gesturing toward the door.

"Think about what you're doing, Mayson," my mom has the audacity to sound emotional right now.

"I have. Believe me, I've thought about what I'm doing a lot."

She steps closer to me, talking quietly. "If he ever pressures you into anything you don't want..."

I bark out a loud laugh. "Trust me, I've wanted everything, but I'll spare you the details."

"Is that all then? You came here to tell us you're not cutting us off *yet?*" Colin asks them both.

I shake my head at the ridiculousness of this entire visit. "So glad we all cleared this up. Don't let the door hit you on the way out."

"What happened to you?" my mom asks, acting like she actually cares.

"Nothing happened to me, it's just who I am."

Colin drops his head to my shoulder, turning to speak directly into my ear. "And who I fell in love with."

I try to bite back my smile, but don't miss the way our parents are looking at us with disgust and disappointment. I can tell they want to say more. Instead, they make the right choice and leave.

The air feels better with them out of our space, and I turn toward Colin. "Are you worried about that?"

He shakes his head confidently. "No. But don't worry, if they try to do anything to ruin your senior year, I'll take care of it."

"You're not killing anyone," I scoff.

"I'd kill for you if that's what it took, babe. I'm crazy about you and *for* you."

"I think you're just plain crazy."

"I think you're right about that." He pulls me against his chest. "I'll show you just how much, but first I want you to run."

My lips quirk in the smallest smile, ready for this game.

Even if everything crashes down around us, I can count on my crazy stepbrother to have my back.

And to fuck me senseless. So, I do what he says and I run.

EPILOGUE

COLIN

HALLOWEEN A YEAR LATER

Being apart from Mayson was not exactly what I wanted, but she insisted on finishing her senior year, and the closest team that offered me a contract was in Vancouver, Canada. It's only about a three hour drive, but it's as far as we've ever been. Though, I still come to her every free moment I have.

But between her school and soccer schedules and my own pro soccer schedule it's been longer than I would prefer. Because we should be together every single night. And we will be, soon enough.

I knew I had to get back to Seattle for Halloween because it's my girls favorite holiday. The best part is she doesn't know I'm coming back for it.

She may think I stopped my obsessive ways, but I never

will. I still know her schedule and have her location on my phone, so I can see she's still at school after practice as I wait in the townhouse she's still living in.

Our house.

Because I started paying for it as soon as I got my first paycheck from the league. My dad can't hold anything over us. We've barely talked to them, but neither of us care. They can support us or they can fuck off. No one else has an issue with our relationship and even if they did, they can also fuck off.

I keep all the lights off, waiting for her to walk through the front door. My skull mask in place.

A new one since my last one ended up being left on the forest floor.

I'm shirtless in shorts that are short enough to show my thigh tattoo I know drives Mayson crazy, along with the silver chain resting against my chest. I know what she likes, and I always aim to please.

The click of the lock on the front door signals her arrival. She walks in, oblivious to what's waiting here for her. She turns on the entry light, kicking her shoes off and walks further inside. As soon as her eyes land on me she jumps.

"Holy fuck, what're you doing?"

I don't say anything, just tilt my head to the side.

She plants her hands on her hips. "We aren't doing this. Use your words."

I shake my head slowly.

She groans, throwing her head back. "Oh for fuck's sake, Colin. Aren't we over this shit?" She turns and starts to walk away, but I'm up, out of the chair, and at her back, caging her in against a wall. She pushes against it, which only has her pushing her ass into my cock that's dying to get inside her already.

"You came home with quite the attitude, figured you'd be happy to see me," I growl against her ear.

"And I figured my boyfriend would greet me instead of sitting in the dark like a creep."

I thrust against her because there's something about her calling me her boyfriend that does it for me. Just like when she says she loves me and calls herself mine. Really, anything she does.

Even when she's acting like a fucking brat like she is right now. It still does it for me.

"You like it," I tell her, and the way she wiggles her ass against me, I know that's true.

"I missed you." She drops her head back against my shoulder. "And I just want to see you."

"I missed you too, but it's Halloween."

"And?"

"And you know what that means." I snake my hand under her shirt onto her stomach, and push her back against me, grinding against her ass.

"It's our anniversary?" she jokes. We don't have an official anniversary and if we did I would say it's the first day I saw her.

I chuckle. "Not quite, baby deer."

I turn her around, pinning her hands up above her head while I keep her pressed against the wall.

Her brown eyes look up at me, wide and full of that fire I love so much. She can't see anything but my own and I know she can see the same reflected back to her.

"Can we not just have one sweet reunion after being apart for a couple weeks?" she pouts.

"You don't want sweet." I don't miss the smirk she tries to bite back.

"What if I just want to kiss you? I can't with this thing on."

"You want a kiss, baby deer?"

She nods, and I can't help but huff out a small laugh.

"Fine." I lift the bottom of the mask, leaning forward and grazing my lips over hers. She meets the contact roughly, her teeth sink into my bottom lip and I groan.

She manages to push me back enough for her to escape and I see the mischievous look all over her face, as she backs up away from me. I fix the mask on my face as I start to stalk toward her.

"Seems like you do want to play," I taunt. "Then let's play."

She turns around, and runs. And just like I always have and always will. I chase her.

THE END

READ THE REST OF RED CARD ROMANCE

Fake & Foul by Octavia Jensen - A Fake dating soccer romance

Bend & Break by Genna Black - a spicy murder mystery soccer romance

Also by Madi Danielle

Uncaged Duet

A dark MMA why choose romance

Uncaged Desires

Uncaged Obsessions

Amity

Small town romances

Embers of You - A firefighter romance

Scars of You - A neighbors enemies to lovers romance

Memories of You - A second chance romance

Denver Dragons Series:

Hockey romances

The Hat Trick - A why choose romance

The Power Play - A forced proximity cam girl romance

Cross Checked - A friends to lovers novella

The Break Out -An enemies to lovers brother's teammate romance

The Falling series

When They Fell - A friends to lovers romance

Who They Are - A cop romance

What They Feel - An enemies to lovers age gap romance

Signed Books available on my website:

www.madidaniellewrites.com

ACKNOWLEDGMENTS

First of all, huge shout out and thank you to Octavia and Genna for doing this shared world with me. We had this planned for MONTHS and I'm excited it finally happened. You guys are the best. Red Card Girlies for life!

Maeghen - As always thank you for beating me into writing and talking me through all my breakdowns.

My Booha, Ashley - You hear every unhinged thought in my brain and want more of it. You keep me going on every single book.

Chelsey - Thank you for your soccer knowledge and also talking me through every break down I have. Also being the best PA in the entire world, duh.

Anja - Thank you for your beautiful graphics and making my social media gorgeous even if it pains you when I go rogue sometimes...sorry.

Thank you to my early readers Blair, Court, Trinity, Lanae and Randi I am so glad you loved these two unhinged babes, I'll have more for you soon ;)

Thank you to Kim as always for the gorgeous book cover. I never make it easy for you, yet you create magic every time.

Thank you to my amazing editor, Kay, I always throw everything at you and you have yet to yell at me. Even though you probably should.

Thank you to all my beta readers for sticking with me and

my tight deadlines on this one you guys are rockstars. Thank you so much to every reader that has ever picked up a book of mine. I appreciate you more than you can ever know. I have many more stories planned, and I can't wait to share them with you all.

About the Author

Madi is a romance author, wife and mother to one daughter and several animals. When she isn't reading or writing you may find her watching hockey or some cheesy movie. Madi has been writing since she was a teenager, but it took a backseat when she went to college and got her degree in Family and Human Services. After working as a social worker, she got back into writing as an escape and hasn't looked back since. Madi is originally from Arizona, but moved to Oregon to attend UO, which is where she still resides with her family.

🅾 📘 ♪ @

www.ingramcontent.com/pod-product-compliance
Lightning Source LLC
Chambersburg PA
CBHW020129120726
47903CB00007B/2178